"Not Only Are You A Fraud...

"...and much too good-looking for anyone's good, but you have a glib tongue, and my mother has always warned us girls about men with glib tongues."

He stuck out his tongue, then said, "It's an ordinary tongue. Why would you think it glib?"

"Glib-tongued men talk women into all kinds of things."

"Like what?"

"Like picnic lunches on a lakeshore and carrying along sleeping bags to 'sit on,' though everyone knows they have ulterior motives."

"I never realized redheaded women could be so logical and knowing. How did you figure out I was trying to have my wily way with you?"

She considered that for a moment, then replied quite logically, "I was trying to help you."

Dear Reader:

Welcome! You hold in your hand a Silhouette Desire—your ticket to a whole new world of reading pleasure.

A Silhouette Desire is a sensuous, contemporary romance about passions, problems and the ultimate power of love. It is about today's woman—intelligent, successful, giving—but it is also the story of a romance between two people who are strong enough to follow their own individual paths, yet strong enough to compromise, as well.

These books are written by, for and about every woman that you are—wife, mother, sister, lover, daughter, career woman. A Silhouette Desire heroine must face the same challenges, achieve the same successes, in her story as you do in your own life.

The Silhouette reader is not afraid to enjoy herself. She knows when to take things seriously and when to indulge in a fantasy world. With six books a month, Silhouette Desire strives to meet her many moods, but each book is always a compelling love story.

Make a commitment to romance—go wild with Silhouette Desire!

Best,

Isabel Swift
Senior Editor & Editorial Coordinator

LASS SMALL
Blindman's Bluff

Silhouette Desire

Published by Silhouette Books New York

America's Publisher of Contemporary Romance

To our eagle-eyed readers:

As you'll soon discover, the title of this book is an
intentional play on the words "blindman's buff,"
and not an editorial error.

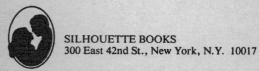

SILHOUETTE BOOKS
300 East 42nd St., New York, N.Y. 10017

Copyright © 1988 by Lass Small

ISBN: 0-373-05413-0

First Silhouette Books printing March 1988

America's Publisher of Contemporary Romance

Printed in the U.S.A.

Books by Lass Small

LASS SMALL:

When I wrote *Blindman's Bluff*, I had no intention of writing a continuing character, but Tate caught my imagination. Why was she at that fishing lodge in Canada? Because I was curious, Tate is in *Goldilocks and the Behr* (a Desire to be published in late summer 1988), which is about her sister Hillary. But I plan to give Tate her own book soon!

With a tip of my hat and a
respectful nod to Iris Johansen, for her
devotion to the continuing character in
category books

How It All Began

——

Probably the most intriguing game of all, and one peculiar to the human race, has been the temptation to direct the lives of those following. So it was that, in Vietnam, Gus Miller and Mac Pederson had set up the legacy.

After Gus had been informed that his beloved wife had safely borne his daughter, Mac and he were well on their way to getting pie-eyed drunk, and they decided to pair up Gus's newborn Kimberly with Mac's five-year-old Logan.

When Gus and Mac were sober again, the kernel of the night's wisdom had remained. Their children would meet and marry, and the two friends would share grandchildren.

But... Who would direct the meeting if both fathers were killed? That was something to consider.

They decided to arrange the meeting, just in case. Since they were directing their children's lives, it all took a great deal of planning and much time.

When should the meeting be scheduled? They pondered that one. Gus finally made the decision: "June. In twenty years. Kimberly will be on summer vacation from college."

Mac added, "Logan will be twenty-five or -six. Ready to settle down."

Where should the meeting take place? Eventually Gus's memory of a fishing resort in Canada held sway. "It's isolated. They'll *have* to talk to each other."

Mac could see that and agreed, "Every evening."

Gus shook his head. "No. We have to designate specific time. How about eight hours together out of every twenty-four?"

They debated and finally decided to require no more but no less than six hours of daily conversation.

The problem was, how could they lure their children into attending such a meeting? Both men knew that two dead strangers saying, "Do it," wouldn't hold much weight. What would tempt their children? Money.

Men in service gamble, and the two were fairly skilled. They began to be a little more careful and saved their winnings, in order to create a legacy for their children to split. It would be the carrot to get them to meet.

There was another reluctant participant in the same war who was a lawyer. It was he who explained how to set up the legacy, he who held their winnings and kept notes on the restrictions governing the children's conduct. By then the rules included penalties for leaving early or for not showing up at all.

The lawyer inquired, "How long should they have to stay there? It'll have to be more than just a weekend."

They settled on two weeks.

The planning entertained Gus and Mac for the rest of their abruptly shortened lives. The lawyer was killed soon after that, but he arranged to send the notes and the money on to his father's firm, and his brother kept track of the legacy.

One

Twenty years after the legacy was plotted—on an innocent spring day in Galesburg, Illinois—two registered letters were delivered to the Lane house. With memories filling her, Ellen Miller Lane read an aged note from her dead husband: *If you're reading this, I'm not there. Damn.*

It was a while before Ellen read her copy of the legacy. For a pensive time she held the second envelope, then put it on the tray in the hall.

At almost three that afternoon Kimberly Miller returned from her classes at Knox College. She was twenty-one, and, like Gus Miller, she was redheaded with green eyes. Kim took one look at her mother and asked, "What's up?" And Mrs. Lane handed her the other envelope.

They went into the living room as Kim studied the return address. "Lawyers?"

"See what it says." Mrs. Lane sank down on a rocking chair by the front window to watch her daughter.

"Well, for pete's sake! Do you know what this says?"

Ellen Lane nodded vulnerably as she looked up at this child of Gus Miller.

Kim frowned. "A legacy. With rules. I've never heard anything so stupid in all my life!"

"I do agree it was unusual," her mother replied softly.

"What possible purpose does this serve?" Kimberly demanded with her own purpose, for she was logical.

Mrs. Lane guessed, "It...would be...interesting?"

"To whom?" her daughter inquired with some coolness. "It's all very well for our fathers to've made this pact before they were killed in Vietnam, but I think it was really rotten of them to have contrived such a weird legacy."

"Riding on this is something like ten thousand dollars—invested over twenty years ago. Do you have any idea of the tidy little fortune involved?"

"From gambling." Besides being levelheaded and logical, Kimberly was virtuous and law-abiding.

"At least your father, and his good friend, Mac Pederson, weren't dope smugglers." Kim's mother watched her. "There wasn't a whole lot to entertain them in Nam."

"But to try to direct our futures from back *then*? It's a time bomb."

"They were best friends, and in Nam that meant a lot. It was years ago now, but they were part of a strange time, and their friendship was all they had. Mac already had Logan, and then you were born. They must have decided it would be very nice to share grandchildren." She smiled mistily. "They were probably a little drunk and feeling exquisitely sentimental."

Kim exclaimed indignantly, "Grandchildren! I'm still in college!"

"Gus meant to guide your life."

Kim's voice softened. "Gus Miller never even saw me. Bob Lane has been my father all this time. I'm really not a Miller; I'm a Lane. It seems very peculiar to have a stranger from twenty years ago reach out of the past and put this burden on me."

"Gus may never have seen you or held you, but don't ever think your father was a stranger to you. He loved you very much. The way Mac loved Logan. Logan's opening an envelope today, too. I wonder what he's thinking."

"He's wondering what—I'm quoting, mind you, so this doesn't count—what the *hell* his father was thinking, to do anything this idiotic."

With time-zone changes, it was earlier in the day at the stucco Pederson house in Sacramento, California. At that moment Logan Pederson said, "What the bloody hell was he thinking? Not too clearly—that's certain! My God, what a stupid thing to do."

His mother shrugged. "They were probably drunk."

"I have to be with her for two *weeks*? I'll bet she's awful."

"Well," Mary Pederson pointed out succinctly, "you don't have to marry her. You just have to spend two weeks at the resort."

"I have to be around her for two weeks!" He said it again because it seemed a very long time to Logan.

"She could be quite plain. Gus was a carrot top, as I recall. His eyelashes and eyebrows were so pale you couldn't see them, and he was skinny."

"Sounds like his daughter would be very exciting." Logan was disgruntled.

"Face it. You can't turn down this legacy. Two weeks aren't much time to spend for half of the money. All they asked was the two weeks. Either it's going to be split between you at the end of that time, or the shares will go to the veterans' hospital. Your choice. If she shows up and you don't, she still gets a quarter of the whole; the rest then goes to the hospital."

"It was stupid."

"I agree. I could've used the money back then. Five thousand was a lot of money at that time, with a little boy."

Logan glanced at his mother. "If you'd had the money then, you might not have started your business. You'd have met some jerk and married him, and where would you be now?"

She smiled at her only child. "We'll look at it your way. If I'd known Mac had that much money and did this dumb thing, I'd never have forgiven him. As it was, I loved him, un-disillusioned. I compared every man to him—not realizing Mac was flawed, mind you—but nobody measured up to him. He was a man.''

Logan wondered if his father was really as great as his mother remembered or if the years had faded Mac's faults. He drank, and he'd been a part of this stupid business. That was hardly a salute to good judgment or stability.

Mary commented, ''You'll have a tough time of it in those two weeks. You're a good catch even without the money. You're nice looking, twenty-six, with a graduate degree, a good job—you could rock her back on her heels. You be careful that she doesn't fall in love with you.''

''No problem.'' He grinned. ''I'll be a nerd.''

''You'd have a tough time doing that.'' She said it with a mother's conviction.

''It'll be an interesting test.''

''I still feel a little sorry for the girl. This will be awkward for her. She's from a little town in the Midwest, and more than likely she's untraveled and shy. Be careful of her; be careful *for* her.''

''Two weeks . . .''

Meanwhile, in Galesburg, upstairs at the Lane house, Kimberly was discussing the situation with her two younger half sisters, who were slouched on the bed in one bedroom. Kim was pacing and gesturing. ''He's probably a klutz who can't put two words together. What will I do with him for *two weeks*? I hope my father is roasting to a turn to have put this off on me."

Nineteen-year-old Janet watched Kimberly thoughtfully. "You're going to have to be careful of him. He *is* from California, and they can be strange, but he might be very sensitive. You'll have to be sure he doesn't fall in love with you and make the rest of his life miserable, when you can't endure him."

On the bed, Pat turned over and sat up. "A disguise!" she exclaimed as if that had never been tried and was a new idea for the universe.

"How?" Janet asked impatiently. "How can Kim possibly disguise herself? Put a paper sack over her head?"

"A wig?" Pat was only sixteen. She sat there in soft jeans, almost lost in an outsized shirt, with her hair mousse-spiked and in three colors. She looked unusual.

Since a logical person can accept reality, Kimberly was fully aware of how she herself looked, so she agreed, "The idea of a disguise does have merit."

Although Pat gave Janet an irksomely smug glance, Janet was unseeing as she speculated, "How do we know he isn't . . . an ax murderer?"

Kimberly nodded one sober nod. "There is that. While we know my father had to be fairly stable, *someone* thought up this weird legacy. The mentally deranged perpetrator must have been Logan's father."

"The resort in Canada is isolated." Pat's voice was slow and dramatic. "There'll be deep woods and probably chain saws.'' She covered her face with her hands.

Kimberly gave her younger sister a withering look—which had no effect—and she scolded, ''I don't need something else to intimidate me.'' When her sisters finished their burst of laughter over the idea of anything intimidating her, Kim went on, ''I need only positive suggestions. What shall I take? What'll I wear?''

Janet was instantly positive. ''Anything of Pat's will camouflage your shape.'' But then Janet added less certainly, ''What if he's a dream, and you fall madly in love? There you'd be, looking just like Pat—no offense, Pat.''

They considered the improbability of Logan Pederson being a dream, before Kim said in her no-nonsense way, ''I'm not interested in a man. I have plans for my life that don't include any man. Maybe in fifteen years I'll consider one, but not until then.''

''A couple of your regular things, just in case?'' Pat suggested.

''No. No reason.'' Kim dismissed the idea.

''Do you ever think of Dad being your stepfather?'' Janet questioned. Although all three had always known, before this strange legacy, the difference in fathers had never been anything but a fact.

''Yeah,'' Pat joined in. ''Especially after he's scolded you?''

Kim shrugged. ''I've had only him as a father, and he's always been good to me. My own father couldn't have been better. Prof. Lane also has very nice daughters.'' She smiled at her half sisters.

Pat guessed shrewdly, "You're saying that now because you think this Pederson guy may really *be* an ax murderer, and you'd want—" As Kim picked up a glass of water, Pat yelped, "No!" But Kim didn't actually throw the water, so Pat just laughed.

When they'd settled down, Janet suggested, "You know, Kim, if you really wanted to disguise yourself, you could do worse than mimic Pat. You could color your hair the way she does, but you'd have to do something about your eyes."

"Dark glasses?"

"What about nighttime?" Pat questioned. "You can't stumble around dark nightclubs with dark glasses. You'd break your neck, and what excuse could you use for wearing them?"

"This is all a real pain." Kimberly raised her arms and let them drop. Then in resignation she asked Pat, "May I borrow some of your things?"

"Okay. If I can wear your clothes."

"Not the spangled dress," Kim cautioned.

"Think what you can do with that much money!" Janet, too, was practical. "All you have to do is last just two weeks, and you'll get a year's good salary! In two weeks! It's worth it."

But Pat leaped up and ran for the door as, out of range, she said, "Not if he has a chain saw!"

In Sacramento, over lunch in a busy restaurant, Logan was discussing the situation with his friend Dan. "It's way off in the woods—our fathers' idea of a good place to be. The trustee said Kimberly's father, Gus Miller, had been there once. It's safe, private, away from the world. Having been raised by Mary Pederson—a self-employed widow—I was never out like that.'' He enunciated carefully, ''What does one do?''

Dan gestured as he spoke. ''Fish, swim, freeze. Those lakes up in Canada stay cold all summer. Take some warm clothes. And mosquito repellent. Want me to go in your place? Kimberly Miller has no idea what you look like. I'll submit my time and energy and body for half the loot.''

''Thanks, but I can't even let you go along. That's specified in the rules and regulations those two set up. I can't take friend, lover or any family along. I have to devote the entire time to her.''

''I'm curious,'' Dan remarked.

''I have to admit I dread it. I'm not in the market for a wife, and you know that's why our fathers planned this meeting.''

''I'll call you about the second day. I'll go crazy thinking she's gorgeous and takes you straight to bed. Nubile, eager—my God!''

Logan laughed. He'd had some thoughts of a transparent negligee over a soft, rounded body; reaching, hungry hands; and a greedy mouth. His smile still wide, he agreed with snide irony, ''Sure. That's how these things always work out, like blind dates turning out to be gorgeous and sex starved. Having that happen is like hitting a lottery. Being hit by lightning's surer.''

Dan offered carefully, ''I could take care of Meg for you while you're away. After all, you'll be gone two whole weeks.''

"Meg and I haven't been together in some time."

"Oh? You're free?"

"Yes," Logan assured his friend. Then he added with emphasis, "And so is she."

"Well, now. Have fun. I'll see you when you get back." He grinned, then belatedly added, "Don't forget to report."

"You won't have time to think about it."

Dan laughed.

And in Galesburg, at the Swanson house, Kim watched as her best friend worked to put blond streaks in her hair. Molly was using a crochet hook to pull strands through holes in a bathing-cap-type headgear in order for them to be bleached separately from the rest of her hair.

The two young women had been quiet for a time before Molly suggested, "If he's good-looking and you could do it, it would be the perfect time for a discreet affair."

"No."

"Keep an open mind," Molly advised.

"There's nothing more burdensome than having an experienced friend."

Molly gave her a heavy-lidded, knowledgeable smile. Kim thought the cap with the wisps of hair pulled through the holes didn't help Molly's steamy look at all.

"You've forgotten," Kim reminded her friend. "I was there right after the Great Seduction, and you said the whole experience was rude."

"That's why you ought to try it next. There has to be more to it than what happened to me."

"If you're so curious, why don't you try it again?"

"I've done my share." Molly acted superior. "It's your turn."

"I'm not that curious."

"I'm about to die of 'curious'! What do you suppose he's *like*? Aren't you going crazy waiting?"

"Not especially. Pat and Janet said that out in the north woods that way he'll probably be a chain-saw murderer," Kim said gloomily.

"That wasn't very comforting. You fly all alone into the wilds of Canada, where there's no way to escape, and they mention a chain-saw murderer. That'll keep you awake nights."

"Thanks a whole lot, Molly Swanson. I needed just that sort of support."

"What do you do at such a place?"

"It's a resort. Those places can be quite posh, even if it is a fly-in. Blue-ribbon cooking, tennis, dancing." Kim paused disgustedly. "He probably can't dance."

"Well, it's only for two weeks. What'll you do with the money?"

"I think I should split it with my sisters. Graduate school. Whatever. There's no reason for me to have it all."

"It's depressing to have you as a friend. You're such a goody. The only reason I don't drop you is I have so much time invested in you, and it would be a nuisance to start over and spend the time to make a friend of someone else."

"I love you, too."

"Logan Pederson. P-e-*d*-e-r-s-o-n. He can't even spell his last name right. If he were from Galesburg, it would be P-e-*t*-e-r-s-o-n, no question. I wonder what he'll look like? I could go along—No, I forgot. No outsiders. How annoying. I'll call you and get the report. Or you call me as soon as you can... I know! Carry a remote phone with you! You can give me an immediate description, a running account as you go along...especially if you decide on an affair. A play-by-play commentary! We can sell the rights and make another fortune. I'll be sitting by the phone in an *agony* of suspense. If you do sleep with him, don't hop right into bed. Be discreet. Wait until the second night."

"Oh, for pete's sake, Molly!"

But Kimberly privately worried. What if he was a slimy horror, even *without* a chain saw? What if he was a leech and she couldn't get rid of him? Two *weeks* of this! Her biological father had some real flaws in his thinking. Maybe it was the emotional ramifications of being trapped in such a stupid war that had warped good common sense, and it wouldn't actually be genetic. Too bad she hadn't been consulted.

The agreed-upon time for the meeting in Canada came the first week in June. Before Janet and Pat drove her to the airport, Kimberly displayed her disguise for all the family. Kim looked more bizarre than Pat, who said it was beginner's luck. Kim's hair was colored in green, black and gold. It was striking. The black portion was pulled up in a moussed sweep and held with black yarn. Her lip gloss was green; on her cheeks was gold instead of blush. She wore black sunglasses. Janet told her she was . . . eye-catching.

Kim's parents looked at her but said very little. Her mother seemed somewhat teary, and her smile wavered. Kim knew her mother was excessively sentimental and this was a touch-back to a different time for her, to the memory of another man, to Gus, who had been her first love. Kim eyed her mother. She couldn't be fighting hilarity, could she? No. It was sentiment.

Kim's stepfather clamped his teeth down on his pipe and made a strangled sound, but Kim knew that he, too, was sentimental. He'd raised her and was sending her off on a rather strange adventure. He was very protective of all his daughters. Everyone said a fond goodbye, and Kim grimly departed on her adventure.

In Kim's travels to Chicago and on north into Canada, no one paid undue attention to her, until the last leg of her journey, where she found a plane waiting. The pilot, Harry, was a big, rough man, and he eyed her suspiciously, as if he really didn't want to fly all by himself—with her—in one small airplane.

In turn, Kim eyed the plane, which looked like a toy with pontoons. It was questionable whether the thing could hold such a big man but impossible that it would hold them both. It did. Her moussed and spray-stiffened hair knocked against the roof of the cockpit, so she had to bend her head a little.

The pilot kept sneaking peeks at her. "You a rock star?"

"No, I'm in school."

"What sort of school?"

Harry sounded as if he would have accepted any kind of weird school. Kim replied, "College. Liberal arts."

"Yeah."

She knew he didn't believe her for a minute. She wished to God she'd just put on regular clothes and forgotten this disguise business. She knew she looked outrageous. If she got to the resort before Logan, she'd use the gel to get rid of the colors and get back to her normal appearance.

Through the plane's window, Kim looked down on an endless expanse of trees. There were no roads. What if they crashed? No one would ever find them. She would be alone with this big man. All her plans for a career would be shattered by the isolation. All alone, she and Harry would be driven by their base natures into each other's arms. Logan Pederson would lead the rescue party to find her, and she would see him as the perfect man; but she would be pregnant and trapped in a loveless marriage for the sake of Harry's child.

Dressed in Pat's clothes, she even thought like Pat! The colors in her hair must be seeping into her skull and addling her brain. She sneaked a look at the silent Harry. What would it be like to make love with such a big man? He'd squash her.

Harry turned and caught her eyes. "You like children?"

She was paralyzed. He was going to suggest . . .

"I got pictures of mine." He reached into his pocket and pulled out a thick wallet that was fat with pictures. He identified every one of them. He had a wife—his size—and five big, strong children.

He didn't look old enough to have that many. Kimberly obediently looked quickly at each of the pictures and wondered how he could take his eyes off where they were go— They were going *down*! They were going to crash! She gasped.

In a perfectly ordinary voice Harry told her, "There it is."

"What? We're . . . there?"

Harry gave her an evaluating look that seemed to question her intelligence.

"The flight was so short," she defended herself.

"We've come quite a ways."

"Really?"

He gave her another dismissing look. "Yeah."

The only place to land was on the lake. He flew just over the water, skimming it, but he didn't slow down! She could see they would hit the dock and splatter among the trees. She braced herself and opened her mouth to scream for him to look out! Then he pulled up, missing the dock and trees.

"You didn't crash!" she gasped.

Patiently spacing the words, he explained, "It's a flyover. I look in the water for logs or anything that'd wreck us."

She could tell that Harry didn't want to be trapped in the woods with her.

As they lifted to circle before landing, Kim saw figures coming to the dock. They wore trousers and plaid shirts like the pilot's. Would Logan be there already? Very late with the question, she asked, "Did you bring anyone else up here today?"

"No."

"Oh."

"Brought a guy in yesterday."

"You did?"

He glanced briefly at her, but then his concentration was on landing. He did it beautifully.

"You're a good pilot," she told him.

"I have to be."

Yeah, she thought. If he made a mistake, he could be trapped in the woods forever with a strange woman of doubtful intelligence who had sculptured moussed hair in three colors and who wore brilliant clothing made for someone a great deal larger than any woman. They'd probably even fit Harry.

They taxied up to the pier and stopped. A scrawny man caught a rope and tied the plane to the pier. The pilot got out and balanced on the pontoon. He turned and looked blandly at Kim. "Brace yourself."

She noticed that Harry had said the words quite loudly, as if he might not be speaking to her.

Harry took her hand, and she ducked so that her stiffened hair would clear the open door. He helped her down onto the pontoon, then led her carefully along it to the pier, where the scrawny man and another waited.

The scrawny one was too old, so the other must be Logan Pederson. He looked so foreign. It couldn't be

Logan. But then the scrawny one asked her, "You Kimberly Miller?"

She nodded and supplied a spoken "Yes," in confirmation.

The scrawny one turned to the other man and said, "It's her, all right." Then he said to Kim, "I'm Jeb. This here's Logan Pederson."

So it was he. He wore thick lenses, and his eyes were enlarged so that he was looking at her as if through magnifying glasses. His hair was parted in the middle and slicked down. He wore a plaid shirt tucked into his trousers, and the sleeves were neatly buttoned at the cuffs. The collar button of his shirt was secured, and he wore a bow tie. With a plaid flannel shirt, he wore a bow tie. Yes, he did. No one would ever have mistaken him for a Californian.

She was kind. As the pilot and the scrawny man watched quite avidly, Kim reached out her hand and said, "How do you do? So you're Mac Pederson's son. We have crazy fathers in common."

He laughed. That set the others off in a jolly wave of hilarity.

Kimberly took her hand back and ignored Logan Pederson's bug-eyed examination. It was, of course, the glasses and not shock that made him look that way. But then her eyes were drawn beyond him, and she stared with a sinking heart.

The word "resort" had given her a false impression. She'd expected tennis courts and a pool, but the forest crowded right up to the lodge. It was not a resort but a large, ramshackle lodge. There were men around who were mostly older. Obviously, there would be no nightclubs and dancing. Subconsciously she'd heard the pilot say something about "...had to see this." And she realized that just before he'd spoken, the scrawny one had asked if his plane was okay.

Logan's vision was distorted, but he saw that she was very young. She had the most fragile neck. Her green lips were perfectly shaped. What color were her eyes? That hair! He doubted she'd be dull. He had a hard time controlling a laugh, and he relaxed.

Her sunglass-protected eyes came back to the magnified, very intent ones of Logan Pederson, who was smiling. At least he seemed a cheerful man. She said companionably, "I believe they are rather casual here."

Logan nodded.

"You came in yesterday? How's the food?"

"Equally casual. The cook's drunk."

"Still...today?" Kim was surprised.

"He's locked himself in the shed until he wants to come out or until he runs out of liquor."

"How nice." She was being insincere.

"We've been warned it might be a week before he's functional."

"I see. And...we are committed to staying here...for two weeks."

"Yes." He slid his hands into his trouser pockets, unaware how marvelously his body moved.

Kim was aware. She considered that contact lenses and hair styling could do wonders for him. But the buttoned shirt and bow tie indicated a strange self-protection.

He'd been well raised, she discovered. He'd automatically reached out a hand to help her along the rough walkway, a well-trodden path. She wondered if there was indoor plumbing. She'd gone to Girl Scout camp once, and there'd been only outdoor privies. It seemed certain to her that she was going to earn every damned penny of that money—the hard way.

The several other guests of the lodge were obviously friendly. Judging from their sizes, she saw that they were mostly older men in their forties and fifties who had gathered to watch the plane's arrival. Or maybe there was nothing else to do? It didn't say much for the next two weeks if the arrivals and departures were the high points in entertainment. That was undoubtedly the case, because they only stared.

Harry and Jeb, the scrawny man, carried her luggage. They had to be sharing some joke, since they chuckled as they followed her and Logan. No one else said anything. Then she remembered how she was dressed and how she must look to these strangers. They were shocked! She was a *spectacle*! Kimberly Miller was a figure of fun?

How rude of them to stare. She gave them all a cool snub.

Logan Pederson didn't release her arm or draw away from her. He was a gentleman. Of course, he was from California and nothing really startles people who live in California. And...ah, yes—*and* he had a lot to gain from being kind to her. He had all that money coming if they both stayed the whole two weeks. If one or the other left, the money gained was cut to a quarter for the remaining one. It was only smart for Logan to be courteous.

Two

When Logan had arrived, the previous day, he'd been surprised the resort was so rustic. Constructed of wooden slabs and stone, it was like the backwoods lodges in paintings people buy to hang on their walls. Not too many people stay in such lodges, out in the middle of nowhere, because those places can be too basic to be comfortable.

This lodge had a large porch across the front, with rocking chairs lined up along the railing, and an old-fashioned iron triangle to be rung for a call to dinner or warn of danger. Inside was a big common room with an enormous fireplace and comfortable chairs. Beyond was a dining room, and to one side was a flight of bare sturdy stairs that led upward. The bedrooms were a surprise. The beds were wide, high and comfortable, with fat pillows, woolen Hudson blankets and down comforters. Everything was solid, sturdy and simple. There were no rugs or drapes, just shades. There was no phone, but there was a ham radio.

Somehow Logan hadn't expected the place to be so relentlessly devoted to just fishing and hunting, without alternatives. He'd brought some paperwork with him, but with the rules of their stay, he would have to give time to Kimberly. He wondered what they would find to do in order to pass the time.

The male guests were older outdoorsmen, rugged, vital, nice-looking he-men. Seeing them, Logan had felt...young, and he'd thought that if Kimberly Miller turned out to be a beauty, there could be complications. She would be the only woman there, in that primitive setting. But when Kim's tricolored head came out of the plane, Logan had relaxed. He decided that with her ease and humor, all would be well.

As Kimberly started up the path, dressed in that green-gold-and-black outfit, Logan automatically took her arm. Then he fervently thanked his mother for her grinding determination and perseverance in teaching him his manners. With the heavy lenses, he couldn't see much of anything, and he used Kimberly as a Seeing Eye...uh...person. She had to move slowly in those heels, and he could go along quite confidently.

For her own safety, it was a good thing she was weird. Of course, in that outfit she could be a raging sex maniac with the morals of an alley cat, and in the next two weeks she could well double her share of the legacy. Who could tell? Some men didn't mind the covering, so long as a female was inside.

Logan allowed the glasses to slide down his nose so he could focus over the top to assess the reactions of the watchers.

He was shocked. They were fascinated. He snapped another look at Kimberly. She looked like some exotic bird who'd been grounded in a barnyard. She didn't look twenty-one, but she *was* of age. That was important, because he needn't be responsible for her conduct. Thank God for that. Those Midwest girls were wild—everyone knew that. They seemed to feel an obligation to refute the Corn Belt image. Obviously, she was a wild one. What a startling outfit. It made her look as if she was willing to try anything.

What if she didn't want to? How far would he be required to go in order to protect her? He looked again at the watchers. Then he glanced quickly at her.

She wasn't a flirt, or at least she wasn't an obvious one. She didn't act coy or swish or wiggle. In those clothes, if she jiggled, who would know? Again he was struck by how young she looked. Was this the right girl? What if Kimberly Miller had sent a substitute? What if she hadn't wanted to come and just paid some stranger to show up? He'd ask to see her driver's license.

"Logan."

Her voice was quiet. Was she afraid? "What?" he questioned. They'd come to the bottom of the porch steps. He wasn't sure how close they were and didn't want to fumble a step, so he waited for her to take the first one, then, holding her arm, he would be able to gauge the step's position.

In the silence, Kim said, "Never mind." She didn't have to ask. Inevitably she would see the plumbing for herself. What good would it do to know now if it *was* outside?

But Logan figured the stares had shaken her and she was uneasy. "You'll be okay." He was pleased his voice sounded positive.

"That's easy for a man to say." She was still thinking about plumbing.

But Logan thought she meant under those circumstances a man would have no reason to be uneasy. Having been raised by a woman alone, Logan knew it was very important that a woman appear confident and in control. He couldn't have Kim be frightened or worried or appearing like a victim. Some men were excited by helpless women. He committed himself with great reluctance, but he really had no other choice. He'd have to help any woman. He said firmly, "I'll be here."

Now, what did he mean by that? she wondered. She concentrated on a review of their conversation and took the first step to the porch. Since she was distracted, she went up the steps like a woman in control. She lifted her chin and gave the porch a cool glance.

The watchers were in the shade on the porch, and, with her dark glasses, Kim couldn't see anything but bulks who were without discernible features. One bulk went to the door and opened it for her. "Welcome to paradise," a deep, attractive voice said to her.

Kim gave a brief nod. She was used to men rushing to her aid. One never encouraged any of them. She went on inside, with Logan in close attendance.

Logan couldn't clearly see the door but didn't hesitate to follow Kim closely so he wouldn't be crowded out by the polite one. Bill—that was his name. He was a menace.

It was odd that Logan suddenly thought of the other men as threatening. They'd all looked fine until she landed. Women were a nuisance. They cluttered up perfectly pleasant times, making situations unnecessarily tense. Without wild Kimberly Miller, there would be no problems.

Speaking of problems, Logan wondered why in hell he'd thought the glasses would be a good idea—*for two weeks*. He should have tried the glasses for a while. Wearing them was dumb. Maybe he took after his father after all.

Jeb and Harry had carried Kim's luggage inside. While the pilot stood as an interested observer, Jeb hurried behind the desk. He grinned, saying, "I'm deskman, too." He owned the place.

Kimberly nodded, accepting Jeb's words at face value. Then she had to raise her sunglasses a bit so she could see under them to sign the register. She put a question mark by car license. There? With no roads, there weren't any cars.

Logan was looking over the tops of his glasses. Her penmanship was neat. Was she really Kimberly Miller? Maybe she was a good forger. She could have practiced the signature. She didn't fidget as if she was guilty of fraud, but anyone who looked like she did could handle the fidgets. She'd probably been a confidence woman since grade school.

He'd heard the screen door squeak open a couple of times and glanced over his shoulder to see that the others were all inside and standing around, watching. He felt bristly. He wished someone would tell the others to get along and mind their own business. Who? Jeb? Hardly. Yollie, the drunken cook? Impossible. Him? He hoped not.

Never before had he *ever* felt uncomfortable in the presence of any other person. He'd never experienced anything like this ominous feeling that *thrummmbed* along his nerve ends.

He couldn't hear any sound from the men, standing there behind them as Kimberly registered. The men hadn't been chatty yesterday or this morning, but they had talked. Now no one said anything, and they didn't move, but Logan could feel the threat of their dormant male power.

They were all older than he by a chunk of years. They were abrupt, basic men who were woodsmen and hunters. How safe was Kimberly Miller in that isolated place? How safe was he? What had their stupid fathers gotten them into? If anything happened to Kimberly, he would be right in the middle of it—and all alone. It could be dangerous. Besides him, she would have only Jeb, the scrawny old man who was owner/caretaker, and Yollie, the drunk locked in the shed.

Jeb got the key to Kimberly's room and handed it to her. Logan looked at the lens-distorted key and considered locking her in her room for two weeks. He was thinking how to do that, when her luggage was suddenly in alien male hands. They were all going to escort her to her room? That wasn't a good idea. They'd get her there and— "Thank you anyway," she said coolly. "We can manage." Ignoring their protests, she took the luggage, handed Logan two cases to carry and took up the rest herself. She did it that simply.

Taking the lead, she marched up the stairs. As he bumped his shin on one step, she turned and waited for him. He felt clumsy. She appeared to be benignly supervising him. He wasn't sure he liked that attitude from her. Out of the edge of his glasses, he glanced back down into the common room and saw the looks on the men's faces as they watched her on the stairs. She had great legs. He took a firm grip on the handles and strode belligerently up the stairs, but at the top, not seeing clearly, he took one step too many and stumbled awkwardly. Damn.

"Here we are." Kim helpfully gave him directions so he wouldn't go on past her. He was blind as a bat. Poor man. Compared to the others, he seemed young. She opened the door onto a snugly crowded room. It was dominated by the bed, but there was a sturdy dresser, a freestanding wardrobe instead of a closet, a chest and large bare windows. She sent a lightning look around the walls. There was no extra door. No bath. Two weeks! She asked Logan for denial, "No bath?"

"Down the hall at the back, on the right. No tub, just a shower—" then he remembered she was female "—washbowl and a john."

"Inside!"

"Yes. Civilized." As he'd spoken, he'd taken off the damned glasses and rubbed his eyes. He was facing away from her and looked around the room.

She told him kindly, "I'm over here."

He turned to look in her direction in some surprise.

"Are you nearsighted?" A stupid question, she chided herself then. He'd hardly wear anything like those glasses if he wasn't! But she wanted to mention his sight problem, and that seemed the easiest way. Her smile was friendly.

"Yes." He went closer to her, reluctantly replacing the glasses. He examined her through those lenses. "You have a lot of teeth."

"Just the usual number." Impulsively, she treated him like all the young males who came to their three-daughter house and hung around. He seemed awkward around her. Some males were. She went on in the same vein. "And you're safe. I have no vampire genes at all."

"Thank God for that."

In spite of the bow tie, he was built very well for a man his age—he was twenty-six—and he must be in reasonably good physical condition, because he'd carried her two cases up the steep stairs with no effort. That was always a clue. He was, what, six feet? Maybe a little more. His hair was very black, and his eyes were blue. The glasses made that plain enough.

"Do you always wear dark glasses?" He was studying her.

"Yes."

"Why? Drugs?"

"Not with my family!" Why *did* she wear colored glasses? She should have figured out something ahead of time. "I have . . . sensitive eyes."

"You shouldn't wear such dark ones. What color are your eyes?"

"Purple."

He grinned. "Sassy?"

She thought maybe he wasn't so awkward after all. "I haven't had much sleep with end-of-year finals. Would you excuse me? I need to freshen up before supper. When are we served?"

"God knows. Yollie's been drunk two days, and we've all just sort of snacked. Sandwiches, lots of beer . . ." He paused at the door. There was a lot of alcohol at the lodge. That wasn't good. Men were bad enough sober. With them drunk, this could get very sticky. She should probably eat in her room and lock the door evenings. He looked at her blurred image and said, "I'll wait for you at the bottom of the stairs."

"Fine."

Since Kimberly had accepted his words with no reaction, Logan realized she had no sense of danger. It was all up to him. Best not to alarm her. That way she could appear normal. Normal? Wearing that outfit? Well, she could be composed. Logan figured he could hurry her through supper and get her back up to her room before any orgy could begin.

He was becoming paranoid. No one had made any overt move.

Yet.

He went out of her room, closed her door and walked carefully to the stairs. Feeling along the wall, he found the railing and went down with caution. In back of him, in the upper hall, he heard her door open and her footsteps going to the bath. Below him he saw the men were still hanging around. They moved, a little restlessly, but they were waiting for her to come back down. This was going to be a long two weeks. How would it end? Those five men would make a formidable pack.

It seemed to take her forever, but she was coming down the steps only about ten minutes later. The men's breathing picked up! Logan could hear them bre—It was his *own* breath that was audible. He was nervous. He wished to God he could take off his glasses so he could see. He was probably ruining his eyes. He tipped his head down so the glasses slid down his nose and gave him a clear, quick look around. Nobody moved.

Kimberly came down the stairs quite naturally, as if she wasn't on display. She didn't smile or look around with more than a scanning, discarding glimpse, then she came toward him. "Is dinner ready?"

"We'll see." He put his fingers on her arm and resisted clenching them to hold her there safely by him. He directed her into the dining room. There were a great many straight wooden chairs and a long plank table that had been scrubbed to a satin finish. There were no places set on the bare table.

Jeb was in the kitchen and, in his querulous voice, was swearing picturesquely. Since Kimberly headed in that direction, Logan went, too, in order to stay with her. It was then he noted the pack had followed.

Kim stood in the doorway and looked at the shambles of the kitchen. "Trouble?" she inquired neutrally.

"I'm a guide—I ain't no bloody cook."

Kim nodded. "Trouble. If Mr. Pederson and I assist you, we will be reimbursed for our lodgings."

"Right," Jeb grumbled.

"And food." Kim was in command.

"The whole shebang," Jeb promised.

"In writing—now." Kim started hunting for a paper and a pen. One of the following pack quickly supplied her with writing materials.

"Uh..." Logan began his protest. Then it occurred to him that if she was an employee *and the cook*, her position might be safer. At his sound, Kim had turned to him in inquiry, so he explained, "I'm not the greatest cook."

"I can cook. My stepfather insisted. He was adamantly unreasonable that we all learn. He must have known I would wind up in just this situation. I've cooked for church suppers, so you're all in good hands. Logan, you can scrape the plates and load the dishwasher."

He had no choice. If he was to watch over her, he had to be with her; and to be with her, he had to be in the kitchen. Ergo, he worked. What fun.

Having delegated Logan to tackle the piles of dirty dishes, Kim turned back to Jeb. "Do you have an apron? I'm as good as dead if I ruin Pat's—my clothes."

Since the men were there, and idle, she put them all to work. No nonsense. The men were either hungry or intrigued by her, so they complied. But she had to remove the sunglasses. Losing that part of her disguise was dictated by her having to see what she was doing.

Logan saw that her eyes were stunningly green. They went with that segment of her hair.

The pack idea had slowly disintegrated in Logan's mind. At least three were just hungry middle-aged men who were normally curious. However, that left two whose interest was different. Two men cannot be considered a pack. They were Bill and Ned, and they asked directions to garner Kim's attention.

It was Logan who helpfully supplied the replies. His mother had taught him housework and kitchen work from age zero, so he knew how to do things. Bill and Ned gave him patient, disgruntled looks, which he didn't "see." The glasses solved that. He saw that Jeb sat on a stool and watched the martinet who was in control. It was clear that Kim knew exactly what she was doing, and they all did as she directed. It's always exhilarating to see someone doing a job well. She said to Jeb, "Check the generator. There's no way in this world we're going to do this accumulation of dishes by hand."

"Yes, ma'am!" He went out to the shed, checked his generator on one side and knocked on the other until Yollie sang a verse or two of something vulgar. Then Jeb got a beer and sat in the shade until it was time to eat.

He almost missed dinner. When the time seemed right, he went inside to find them all at the table. It was nicely set, and everyone was eating. He found a chair and sat down. He was given a plate and told, "Take it to Yollie."

"He don't eat when he's drinking."

Kim lifted those green eyes to Jeb's, clearly expecting to be obeyed, and Jeb found himself outside, going to the shed, where he rattled the doorknob. "Yollie, here's your supper."

"Zuper? Who's da cook? You?"

Yollie had never really learned to speak English. Jeb could understand him and readily interpreted for him. He replied, "No. A lady guest."

"Watzit?"

It was then that Jeb looked at the plate. There were chops, vegetables, apple sauce and thick biscuits with honey already soaking in. He ate half a biscuit. Chewing, he said, "I think we hit it lucky, and you might never get out of there."

"Wars zit?"

"Here you go, you old goat." Jeb slid it through the bottom of a nailed window, then stood and listened. Soon came the sounds of eating. They couldn't allow Yollie eating utensils at such a time, so he ate with his fingers. If Yollie began to eat, he might be out in a day or two. Jeb's eyes narrowed. They could nail the door shut.

Jeb hurried back to the dining room to see the meat platter was empty, and so was the biscuit tray. Indignantly he protested, "My—"

"Sit down, Jeb. I have your plate warming." Kim got up and went to fetch it herself.

During the meal, the people were sorted out. Jennings, Morris and Patrick were the middle-aged visitors. It was Bill and Ned who were the remnants of the pack.

Everyone scraped his own plate and loaded it in the dishwasher. That way they could go past Kimberly. They could look at her, this strange creature from another planet who cooked like a dream. They wasted smiles and compliments. She began to mix dough. The two hung around, leaning on things, getting in Logan's way. Kim set the bread to rise, washed her hands, and they all trailed after her into the common room.

One of the older men asked, "We know you and Logan are here because your fathers made the plan for you to meet. Logan told us. Why not before this?"

Logan replied for her, "The whole thing baffles us. They were good friends. I suppose they wanted us to be friends."

"To marry?"

Logan opened his mouth, but Kim replied, "No."

"Why not?" Bill was the one who asked.

"I'm still in college." Kim gave a level look. "I have another year at Knox. Then I'm going to graduate school. I haven't time to be serious. And from what I understand, Logan doesn't, either. He's just begun a demanding job."

They weren't interested in Logan and let the opening pass.

"Why here?" asked the first man. "Why in this place, and for two weeks?"

Logan turned his owl eyes on Kim to keep her from mentioning the money, then he replied, "Mother said they were probably drunk."

Kim laughed. "My mother said the same thing. They were young. Far from home. They each had a child." She shifted and asked, "How about cards?"

They all played, except Logan. He "couldn't see" the cards, but he watched the men, and he saw they were letting her win. They were indulgent and laughed as their scores piled up.

Kim wondered, how does a woman who is twenty-one tell men who are all nearly old enough to be her father that she doesn't have to win at cards? Men are difficult. There she sat, the only woman in a hunting lodge, playing hearts, for pete's sake. Not even poker. Hearts. And Molly had suggested that Kim take the opportunity to have a discreet affair? Logan couldn't see well enough even to find her in an empty room in daylight. He'd been facing the windows when he took off his glasses and looked for her. He had beautiful eyes.

She won yet again. What a bore. She rose and said, "Logan, since you're my escort, would you take me for a walk before I fold up for the night?"

Chairs scraped as the others volunteered. "Sit still," she insisted, confident they would obey. "According to the rules our fathers laid down, we have to spend six hours a day together in conversation."

Logan got up from his chair. "Yes, but it's late. It's almost sunset, and up here, that's after eleven this time of year." He made a vague gesture. He was a city man in a wooded place without sidewalks or streetlights.

"I can see perfectly," Kim assured him. "Let's go." Since his sight was so poor, he probably didn't get enough exercise. She'd have to see to it that he walked and swam. How cold was the water? She turned to the other guests. "I suppose you gentlemen will be up early for the fishing in the morning? I'll have breakfast ready for you. Omelets? Pancakes? Five o'clock? How about six?"

They laughed and agreed to all that, and she asked for enough fish to serve for dinner. They assured her there would be more than enough. She smiled. "There is sausage, but I would enjoy some trout."

So Logan and Kim went out the door and stood on the porch in the gorgeous late sunset. The woods beyond the lodge were thick. There was a wide variety of trees, some reaching sixty feet in height. Logan took off his glasses and put them into his pocket.

She took his hand with great gentleness, and he managed not to laugh out loud in pure male glee. She was going to lead him? How clever he'd been to wear those damned glasses!

"Ah, Logan, I wish you could see this night. It's just lovely. How much can you see?"

"There's a sunset." A nice nonlie.

"It touches everything with gold. It's just beautiful. Come along. I'll help you."

After a while he forgot to stumble. But she didn't forget to warn him, to lead him, and she was so diligent that he figured out she thought it was her skill that made it easy for him.

He liked her small hand in his. She had a pleasant voice, and they talked as they wandered along. The ground was covered with a spongy moss, which made it hard to walk any distance. As they followed the trails, he helped her keep track of where they were by asking for the sequence of landmarks back to the lodge. That way if she got lost, he could recite the landmarks for her as she thought she led them back. He was clever.

"You turn your head." She was merely observing.

She'd caught him looking around. "I listen," he replied gravely, rather amazed he'd thought of it so quickly. "The water is to our right. I'm trying to help keep us located."

"How smart you are! I've always heard when one sense is inadequate, the others become more acute."

Like feeling his hand around hers, he thought. He was acutely conscious of it.

It was very pleasant out there for the two. They moved slowly as they talked of their early lives, their parents, schools, the ordinary things they'd done. Their exquisite consciousness of each other was probably because they had just met. It'd been arranged; therefore, they were more aware of each other.

But the time came when they had to go back, and Kim yawned. "I have to see to the dough. Are you getting up in the morning? Will you go fishing?"

"I'm not a fisherman. I've never done it."

She thought he'd probably been too protected, having grown up with flawed sight, the only child of a widow. He needed ordinary experiences. "I'll teach you how to fish." It was then that she decided to use the time they'd be stranded there together to expand his life. This could be a fulfilling holiday for him.

"So you know how to fish?" He swung her hand a little.

"One can do anything one sets one's mind to do."

He thought she was just a little sassy, and that delighted him. He said, "Anything we set our minds to? Uhhh. Check."

They strolled back to the lodge and found everyone on the porch waiting for them to come back. Not Yollie—he was still in the shed.

"We were worried," Bill said.

Another of the group scolded them, "It's dark out there, and there *are* bears. You have to be careful."

"The way Logan sees, you'd be helpless," Jennings added.

"Logan got along very well," Kim said in his defense.

Logan thought that maybe he'd lucked into something good with those damned glasses. The men considered him no threat at all, and Kim thought him helpless. Good. He smiled.

They all went into the kitchen to watch Kim punch down the dough, form the loaves and rolls, cover the trays and put them into the walk-in cooler. Since the men were there, she had Logan empty the dishwasher and told the rest to set the table for breakfast. They argued nicely and with humor as to who would sit next to Kim in the morning and whether they could get anything off *their* tabs since they, too, were working. There was no answer to that, because Jeb had gone to bed.

Courteously they allowed Kim to use the bath first. After a quick shower, Kim discovered there was no mirror in the bath. The place had not been planned to accommodate women. The men were in the hall when she emerged. She had on sturdy cotton pajamas, which should have been a put-off, but she was quite a bit smaller than any of them, and she was the only woman. They smiled at her.

Logan was leaning by her door and he growled in her ear, "Lock your door."

She gave him a big-eyed look, which she figured was wasted on him, and whispered back, "I'm twenty-one."

Logan went to bed and lay there trying to figure out which she meant: that, being twenty-one, she was her own boss, or that she already knew to lock her door, or that if she wanted company, it was none of his business? He didn't sleep well. He dreamed of the pack chasing Kim and he was really blind and unable to help her.

Three

———

Kimberly had set her clock alarm for four-thirty. She'd slept dead to the world and wakened to the small sound feeling rather groggy. For a good ten minutes, she sat on the edge of the bed, adjusting to reality. But since she'd slept so heavily, when she stood up and stretched, she wakened fully, and she thought: Logan's here. How odd that the thought excited her.

As she dressed, that Saturday morning, in jeans and one of Pat's wild shapeless sweaters, she thought how providential Yollie's session in the shed had been. What would she and the half-blind Logan have done for two weeks? Working would make the time go more quickly, and they'd have another couple of thousand to split at the end of it.

How amazing it was that Logan was endurable. She'd fully expected a real nerd. But he was a very unthreatening, nicely made man. A young man. If she'd met him in his own environment, she'd probably consider him fully grown, but against the other, older men, he was young.

Maybe he was young, but, for all that, he wasn't diminished by the others. He was simply not as old. He moved and appeared confident that he was as good as they. If he could see better, he would be formidable. His body was very well made.

She'd never paid much attention to male bodies before then. How interesting she was conscious of Logan's. She had been aware if someone didn't stand straight or was too fat, but she'd never noticed... maleness before. Logan was a male.

With no mirror in the bath or in her bedroom, Kim used her makeup mirror and did the best she could with the mousse. The colors were semipermanent but could be washed out with a special gel. However, Kim wasn't yet old enough to wash out the colors—and admit she'd disguised herself. Dressed, carrying her shoes, she carefully unlocked her door and tiptoed to the bath. With the water very cold, she washed her face minimally and scrubbed her teeth. She opened the door and walked right into Logan, who was also dressed.

She hadn't expected anyone else to be up yet, and he surprised her. He automatically caught her and steadied her. He wasn't wearing his glasses, so she whispered, "Good morning. It's I, Kimberly."

"I recognized the voice... and you're shorter." He grinned down at her. "And softer."

It was almost as if he could focus. She smiled and said, "Oh, you..." as she made a friendly fist and gave him a tap off his biceps, very pleased they could be so easy together.

She went on downstairs as Logan stood watching after her. He started to go into the bath but became still, to lift his head. She wore a faint perfume. It was a very subtle reminder that a woman had been there. He could barely discern it. He stood, aware of her as a woman. Not as a woman potentially in danger who might need to call on him, but as a woman.

In the kitchen, Kim removed the formed breads from the cooler and set them to rise. She started the large coffee maker, began the pancake batter, the icings for the rolls and the omelet fixings. She set out the meats and put bacon strips on large trays ready to go in the broiler.

Logan came cautiously through the kitchen and fumbled around before he drew himself a cup of coffee. He sipped, then closed his magnified eyes. "You measure!"

She grinned. "Apparently Jeb doesn't?"

"No one knows what he does. And since Yollie was already incapacitated when I arrived, I had nothing with which to compare Jeb's."

"You're a caffeine devotee?" she guessed.

"Who isn't?"

"I escaped."

He leaned back against the counter, in her way, and said judiciously, "When you exited the plane, I suspected you might be different."

For a split second she looked blank, then she re-membered her tricolored hair, remoussed just that morning, and she laughed.

He'd fully expected her to be miffed, to snub him and make him tease her into good humor. Her laugh-ter surprised him, but then, so did her pitching right in to help out with the cooking. Help out? She was doing it all. The way she looked, no one could guess she was a salvager and a hard worker. Here she was, and it was just after five in the morning! Not only that, but she'd included him in the financial benefits of her deal. Interesting. He inquired, "What other talents have you?"

"I'm committed. Right now I'm studying. I'll have a degree in liberal arts next year, then I'm going to get a master's in business, and after that I'll see which way I want to go. I had planned on the master's, but with this money from our fathers, getting the master's is going to make a tough time very easy. It'll be worth the two weeks here."

She hadn't mentioned meeting him as being worth the trip. He didn't think she could "see" him. She was so taken up with her own life and plans she wasn't re-ceptive to alternatives. That piqued him just a little. Women were attracted to him. He wasn't used to being ignored. Not that she ignored him per se; she just didn't seem to be *aware* of him.

"How did you grow up to be twenty-six and never go fishing? That's un-American."

"My mother didn't remarry. After Mac and Gus were killed in Nam, she faced the facts of life, started in interior decorating, expanded, and formed her own company. She's good, works hard, and she's been a great mother. I admire her. I not only love her in the obligatory parent way, but I think she's a special woman who..."

Kim thoughts went immediately to: Uh-oh. Mother fixation. I pity his wife.

"...has done her damnedest for me. We had four exchange students, each of whom lived with us for a school year. Mother wanted me to know other peoples, so I have four 'brothers' around the world. In high school, during spring breaks I went on the student tours to Europe and South America. She did her best to expand me and give me opportunities I might not have had if there'd been brothers and sisters. No siblings was one reason we had the exchange students, and we got some great guys."

"But you never went fishing, even in a kids' camp?"

"Summers I went to Scout camp, swimming camp, tennis camp, basketball camp and then several years of computer camps. But there wasn't ever any fishing. I'm looking forward to your teaching me." And he smiled.

By midmorning, Kim had the kitchen organized so she and Logan had free time. She asked Jeb for two poles with string. He offered rods with reels, but she shunned anything so easy.

"Easy?" Jeb questioned in a very unbelieving way.

"I'm a basic fisherwoman." She took bacon from the cooler and sliced it to her own specifications. "Do you have crickets up here?"

"We'll have a precious many mosquitoes in a couple of weeks."

"They'd never fit the hooks."

"We're going to have hooks?" Logan was indulgent. "I'd almost decided you planned for us to stand in the water and catch the fish with our bare hands, since they'd be lethargic from the cold."

"That *is* one way. However, we are going to fish in the classic manner." She was positive, businesslike, no-nonsense. But then she cut the hooks from the lines!

Jeb screeched, "What the *hell* are you doing?"

She gave him a cool, quelling glance as one does to someone who is behaving in a strange manner. "Classic fishing is always done with bent pins."

"Good God Almighty!" Jeb flung his hat down on the ground.

"That's what I've always heard." Logan supported Kim, which earned him her wide smile.

Jeb silently snatched up his hat and stalked away.

Kim gave Logan the poles to carry, then she efficiently took his hand to lead him along the lake to a likely place. There, they sat, soaking the bacon in the lake, as they exchanged growing-up stories, laughed and didn't catch anything. She asked him about his father.

"I don't believe my mother has ever forgiven the government for sending Dad over there to die so uselessly and so far from home. I have no real memories of Vietnam, so that can't be why I feel so antiwar. It could be mother's bitterness over Mac not coming home, or it could be my own regret for being denied a father, or maybe I'm honestly opposed to any violence. I've never been sure. I doubt I could ever deliberately harm anyone."

"I'm not sure I could. It would depend on the circumstances."

"Kimberly, I find you fascinating." He narrowed his eyes, but remembered he couldn't see and narrowed them to one side of her, but he pretended he felt he was looking right at her. "I believe I'll do a thesis on you. 'The Woman of Today.'"

"First you're going to have to be able to find me. You're looking at a tree."

"Where exactly are you? Your voice is coming from there." He pointed to the tree.

She took his hand and brought it back so that it pointed right at her face. And it seemed to her that he could really see her, his eyes moved over her so carefully.

"Kimberly Miller, the daughter of Gus and... Ellen?"

"Yes, but I was raised by Bob Lane. He's a good man, too."

"I'm glad."

They had their picnic lunch and a nap. Kim had never slept on a blanket with any man, and she was very self-conscious for a while; but he slept, and she found her breathing synchronized with his, and that was the last she knew. She wakened to be surprised it had been so easy to "sleep" with a man, and she smiled. When it was time to start dinner, she gave him the poles, took his hand and led off.

As they walked back toward the lodge, Logan was rude enough to mention they had no fish. She gave him her superior glance, thinking it was too bad he couldn't see it, and replied, "I know. In classic fishing, done by the purists, the actual fish don't matter. It's the exercise, the day and the company."

"I like the way you think."

"Who would want a fish to bite down on a bent pin? Barbaric!" She strode along, watching for the easiest way for his stumbling feet, and he allowed his steps to lag so he could watch her walk.

The fishermen arrived with a generous catch of rainbow trout, which they'd scaled, cleaned and filleted. She admired all the fish and even admitted she and Logan had been out and not caught anything. She was besieged with offers of help, which she declined.

The fillets were lined in pans, and Kim added canned tomatos, lemon juice, a little dill, and covered the pan tightly but punched a hole in the aluminum foil. The pan was placed on smoldering wood coals Jeb had prepared outside, with wrapped potatoes already baking in the hot ashes. There was a table set with utensils near the lake. The men sipped a libation as they waited, whetting their appetites.

When the hole in the aluminum steamed, the fish were done. She served the baked potatoes with sour cream, and a salad and fruit and crunchy rolls. A couple of the men sat at the table, but others separated, going to places where the view was lovely. There they could savor the food while their gazes rested on the beauty of the land. They ate with relish.

Then Kim served three kinds of pie, a custard, a berry and an apple, with the requisite coffee. They played hearts again. Kim declined. She'd decided to read to Logan and began a detective story. The card-playing men could listen, too.

At bedtime, when Kim went to her room, Logan escorted her safely there, and again he told her, "Lock your door."

She groused, "Oh, for pete's sake!" but she did it. He was very protective. She decided it was because their fathers had been friends. Therefore, he felt an odd kind of kinship? There was no other reason for him to worry about her. Too bad he hadn't had any sisters. He would realize women are very capable. They can take care of themselves. Her stepfather had seen to it that his three daughters could handle anything.

The next morning, when Kimberly went down to begin her preparations for breakfast, the men were wakening. As the two younger, single men yawned, scratched and stretched, their eyes came to Kim with shadows of another kind of hunger. The older, married men looked, too, but the look was more of distant appreciation. Male for female.

Logan was surprised to recognize the nuance of difference. Bill's survey of Kim was the boldest. Logan felt his hackles rise. He had no hackles; he was a civilized man. If that was so, why could he feel them rise along his spine? He took some comfort from the fact he didn't actually bare his teeth.

When the men weren't fishing, they took turns splitting logs for the fireplaces. They worked around, doing jobs they were paying good money to be allowed to do. They checked their tackle for the next day, then some of them went down the lake a way and swam naked. They laughed and called to one another, showing off a little as if they hoped Kim was watching.

She wasn't.

The men had invited Logan to go along for the swim, but he'd declined. They'd accepted that easily enough. But Logan found himself restless and wanting to...what? To show off for Kim? That was too juvenile. He had no idea what bothered him, because he'd never felt that way.

In some disgust, he told himself that the men's loud, shouting laughter and showing off was probably a natural, very basic feeling of competitiveness. If that was so, then why did he feel it, too? Did he feel as if he was competing for Kim? Nonsense! They were simply here for two weeks. That would be the end of it.

Then why was he restless? He was impatient with himself and therefore with Kim. She was a female in a male world, and any woman in those circumstances is a nuisance.

The next morning the five and Jeb went off in two boats, leaving Logan with Kim...and Yollie in the shed. With hardly any thought at all, but with some glee, Logan took his glasses out of his pocket, dropped them on the floor and deliberately stepped on them, crushing them. He picked them up and looked at them with intense satisfaction. That had been solved handily. Then Kim came through from the kitchen and saw what had happened. "Oh, no! You do have another pair? Anyone with your problem does, right?"

He remembered to look three feet from her and say solemnly, "My last pair."

"Now what'll you do?"

"I may need a little help." And he managed not to smile.

"Of course. Tell me when you need me."

After that, as he blundered with great calculation, he speculated on exactly how she could help him. And several days passed with the routine becoming solid. She got up at four-thirty, and so did he. She led him around and sorted out what chores he could do seeing as poorly as he did, and he did them. They fished with no success and talked and laughed as they became friends. Every time she went to her room, he made her lock her door. And he continued in his deception of being unable to see well.

Naturally, not seeing, he couldn't play cards. At times, even the men guided him with a word or with a helpful hand. They were completely fooled. He talked to doors or to cupboards and once to a floor lamp, but only Bill narrowed his eyes suspiciously. Then Logan miscalled him Yollie.

That was after Yollie had come out of the shed on Tuesday. He, too, became a happy slave to the woman whose three-colored hair now had red roots. Logan looked at those roots and thought of other decorations that must be that color. He was going to have her. The daughter of his father's best friend.

Then Jeb gave Logan a small round Christmas bell to put on his cork so that he could hear it if the cork bobbed. And, with sly calculation, Logan devised a game.

That day when they went for a session of purist fishing, he just happened to "find" a bell in his pocket as he took out his fishing knife. Hearing it, he invented the game. "We could bell a cat," he said as he made the bell sound.

"I'll tie it on you," Kim volunteered.

"No, I'm not the one who needs a bell. Let's tie it on you so I know where you are."

So then it was only a small verbal jump to "finding" Kim with only the bell to guide him. He was clever. As the corks on their fishing lines sat on the lake nearby, he drew a circle on the ground and they played cat and mouse...or blindman's bluff. That was exquisitely droll, for that was the farce he played.

Out there in that primitive setting, the antiwar man defended the circle, while the liberated woman wore a bell that jingled as she moved.

Logan's hands had been a little careless when he reached to tie the bell on Kim's back, but that was understandable. And she threw herself into the game. She patted his shoulder as she dodged inside the circle and escaped. He played a great sham of being so clumsy and helpless, but the time did come when he finally caught her!

"I got you! I got you!" And he moved his hands quickly, brushing over her. In his eagerness to bind his captive in his arms, he hugged her tightly.

And she was delighted. "Of course, it was a fluke. The damned bell."

"I get a kiss."

"Oh? You didn't mention that in the rules."

"Well, darn, how could I have forgotten to warn you? I suppose I didn't believe I had a chance." His conscience didn't even flinch.

Kim made the requisite struggle. He was still holding on to her as if she might get away. His body was very hard. The odd feelings of being held between him and his hands did strange things to her insides. She squirmed and pushed on his hands, but she wasn't in earnest, and that only tautened her breasts against his strong chest. She rather liked it that his hands became harder and his arms held her fast. It was a game. So she struggled just a little more, and he pulled her closely to him.

She said primly, "Kissing is out." She knew full well he would then insist. What man would give up so easily? She would be kissed. She'd just tease him so that it would be more fun...under these particular circumstances.

If she hadn't wanted a kiss, she would never have agreed to the game. Any woman who agrees to a cat-and-mouse game with a man does it to tease and expects to be caught.

He was teased. And she was caught. She excited him. He knew his eyes were as hungry as Bill's. He didn't want just a kiss. He wanted Kimberly Miller, with her tricolored hair, which now had red roots, and her baggy clothes, which covered a delectable body, as his hands had discovered, and her sassy mouth, which he was going to kiss.

"The cork's down!" she lied. "We have a *fish!*" He wouldn't be able to see if she lied or not.

"To hell with that cork. You're popping mine." His voice was a low growl. His sound surprised him, and he heard her responsive intake of breath. So he bent his head down to kiss her.

He moved his mouth a searching hairsbreadth over her face in a blind search for her lips. The sensation was toe curling for them both, and his kiss was simply remarkable! He hadn't known he was that good. He kissed her, folded her into his arms and prolonged the thrilling sensations that rocked him like an earthquake. His balance was strained, but his feet were braced and he rode it out, with all his muscles tensed to iron.

Kim made a little sound that had his hair standing on end, and her lips softened so their kiss deepened. When at last he finally lifted his mouth and looked down at her, she was dazed. She lay in his arms, unmoving, allowing him to hold her limp weight. He smiled like a pleased wolf, and that, too, surprised him. Was he really such a basic man? Apparently.

He kissed her again, taking her defenseless mouth like a conqueror. He tasted not only a delicious woman but the excitements of a dominant male. He hadn't known how it felt to subjugate a woman. He'd been raised by a feminist and agreed to that, but this was another thing entirely. He was male to her female. It was always so. Whether he conquered her or whether she allowed it, Kim welcomed it. The feelings were so strong that he wanted to put her down on the ground and take her right there. Some safety valves did work, and he resisted, but just barely and only with determined control. He was almost surprised that his control did work. He realized he'd better sort this out. He released Kim, however reluctantly, and with his hard hands he stood her on her feet and steadied her. He said, "I need a swim."

That startled Kim. He was letting her go? Now? When she was mush! Malleable mush! She'd have let... Well, how astonishing! Molly should have waited for someone like Logan. It would probably be just terrific with him and not at all rude. She formed the words with some difficulty: "We don't have our suits."

He laughed in genuine humor. "You can look at me. I'm not modest. Remember, I broke my glasses. You can feel completely confident with me under these circumstances. So, why not?"

Why not indeed? He was always talking to cabinets and doors. He had to be led around. He really couldn't see. So why not? And she was so curious! "I won't peek." He'd never know whether she did or not.

He was indignant. "Do you mean you didn't drag me out here to rip off my clothes and feast your lascivious eyes on my naked body?"

"Did you think that?" A neat nonreply. And her voice had sounded nicely shocked. He couldn't see her smile.

He began to unbutton his shirt. "How far am I from the lake?"

"About thirty feet. Uh, there're some rough places. I'll have to lead you." She'd taken off her top, and, with her strong sense of modesty, she held her shirt to her chest before she reluctantly allowed it to fall.

"Thank you. You'll only touch my hand?"

"I'll restrain myself."

"Well, damn."

She laughed with a delightfully naughty trill as she skimmed out of her jeans.

"Any fig leaves around?" He looked around blankly, swinging his head as if examining the trees, while he slid out of his jeans and started off.

"Not that way," she warned.

"Let's put the bell on you. Then I won't get too far from you and drown. I'm only a mediocre swimmer." He said it blandly. He was a senior lifeguard.

"You want to bell the mouse?"

"Do you consider me a cat?"

"Isn't that what we were playing?"

"Who's playing?"

She was suddenly silent.

"I don't want to get too far away from shore," he told her. "I wouldn't know which way I should go. The water will be cold, and I could cramp. Could you help me then?"

"I took the Red Cross classes. You're safe with me. I'll take good care of you." She put her hand on his and took it.

He was earnest as he reached and brushed her naked breast with its soft nipple. "Let's—oh. Sorry. What a lie. How lovely you must be." He had extremely excellent peripheral vision, so he could intently look off to one side, and she was convinced he couldn't see.

"Behave," she scolded in a gentle voice, not the least alarmed. His body was lovely. Beautiful. Aroused. Did he know? She supposed it couldn't do that without his knowing. He was awesome. And he stood so strongly. How amazing he was. He fumbled to tie the bell to her wrist while she stood still for it. His eyes were concealed by his lashes as he tried to see to tie the strings. Her compassion was touched. With the bell firmly on her wrist, she took his hand and said softly, "Come. Move carefully."

"I will."

"It'll be cold."

"I'll probably steam. Do I shock you?"

"You're beautiful."

"It isn't fair for you to look. I thought you said you wouldn't," he chided.

"I said I wouldn't touch."

"I don't mind if you want to."

"How shocking you are, Logan Pederson."

"I could *really* shock you."

"I think we'd better swim."

"What a cold bucket of water you are," he groused.

"No…step there. Yes. Careful. We're here. Into the lake with you. Don't dive. Wade, but be careful—it could drop off fast."

It didn't. It was shallow for twenty feet and only thigh-high. He laughed. She did, too, and moved her wrist to ring the bell. He went for her. She fled, and he chased her as if the bell led him on. She was astonished he could follow so accurately. And he caught her. He tumbled her into the cold water, and she shrieked at the cold. Then he lifted her to him and kissed her. She was startled over the amazing feeling that burned through her cold body. Fire and ice. She wound her arms around his head, and they steamed, they were so hot.

He lifted his mouth as he slowly rubbed his hairy chest against her hardened nipples, causing a friction that she felt all through her frozen body. He said to her in a low, husky voice, "I want you."

"Nooo..." The reply was so tentative. She said more strongly, "No," but only then did she draw back, or at least she did try to.

"Come up on the bank. I'll get you warm."

"No."

"You're going to spend the rest of your life standing out here in the water? It'll freeze this winter, but you'd freeze before then. This water is cold. Not cold enough to cool me, but we'll get pneumonia if we stand here much longer."

"I'm not going to let you have me."

"Not now," he agreed.

"Not anytime." Kim was positive. "My schedule doesn't include any part of this."

"We'll see." He found that an interesting word choice.

Four

That night at supper everyone expressed elaborate surprise to have fish again. "No imagination," they all teased Kim.

Jeb said crankily, "Since Yollie's out of the shed, Kim should go back to being a guest."

That created a hubbub of protesting conversation, and Mr. Jennings offered to get Yollie a bottle of booze. Little, scrawny Jeb threatened to throw the big, solid Mr. Jennings out the door if he did that. When the hilarity settled down, they decided they'd be democratic—which caused loud protests from two Republicans—and vote on keeping Kim as cook. Even Yollie voted for Kim. They laughed and asked him why he didn't vote for himself. Yollie said a string of words that Jeb interpreted to mean: "I always vote for redheaded women."

"You're a redhead!" Bill's voice was soft.

Although Logan intimately knew she was naturally red haired, hadn't Bill noticed Kim's red roots? Logan wondered how Bill had missed that simple fact. Where had his eyes been? He said to Bill stiffly, "You must be the blind one—her hair's green, black and gold."

"I've wondered if you honestly couldn't see. You've just proved it. It's a beautiful red." Then he said to Kim, "Why'd you put that junk on it?"

"Red is so dull," Kim replied disgustedly. "I colored it so I could have a change." The men exclaimed they liked red hair best, but she groused, "That's because it isn't your hair."

They ate their fish-surprise dinners with savoring sounds and then demolished Kim's pan cake made with thick chocolate icing and served with vanilla ice cream.

They talked so much that it was late when the men rose to take their plates to the kitchen. They groaned, complaining how much they'd gain, when they were up there to lose weight and tone their muscles. Mr. Morris sighed, "My wife will think I went to some really posh resort, and she'll demand to come along next year."

Bill knew she was a young, second wife and said, "Bring her. I'll find ways to entertain her."

"Not you!"

Yollie offered with wicked humor, "I be dah cook 'gin."

They refused his offer in rather imaginative terms, considering they were watching their language with a young lady there.

As they moved about, clearing the table and putting their dishes into the dishwasher, Logan heard Bill quietly ask Kim, "You guys go swimming today? Sound carries across the water, and I thought I heard you laughing. Did you need someone to get you warm again? The water's cold."

"A very quick dip. It *was* cold."

"A quick one is always fun." He smiled down at Kim suggestively.

Again Logan felt his nonexistent hackles rising.

Kim asked Bill, "Didn't you swim last night when you came back from fishing?"

Bill thought, She'd watched? "We... I was hot."

Logan intruded: "So were we."

Bill gave Logan's earnestly averted face a long look, then he said, "Yeah. I'll bet."

But in marking his territory, Logan realized he had inadvertently issued a challenge.

After supper, Kim settled down with the book to read the next two chapters to Logan. The rest of the men moved their card game so they could hear as they played.

The book was a well-paced, violent story, just the kind one would expect to be kept there in the lodge.

Kim read well. Her voice was pleasant, and her pace of reading didn't drone along. When she closed the book after the allotted pages, the men begged for one more chapter, making their pleas with calculation so that they would sound just like kids in a classroom, but Kim was used to kids. She told them prissily that was all, and they were to brush their teeth before they went to bed.

Several of the others went upstairs with Kim and Logan, and Logan wasn't given the chance to kiss Kim good-night. His dreams were tumultuous. So were hers.

The radio had predicted a storm quite accurately, for it blew up wild, windy and very noisy in the night. The bedroom chests were opened and woolen blankets added to the beds. And when four-thirty came, it wasn't easy for Kim to crawl out of her snug, warm nest. She did emerge, for she wasn't sure whether fishermen allowed weather to interfere with their devotion to their sport.

She met Logan at her door. He moved her back into her room and kissed her hungrily and with great skill before he allowed her to release herself from his iron arms and leave him there.

The guests were all late in getting out of bed. Jeb had built a big fire in the common room, and it was fragrant and cozy. Kim was tolerant of the lazy stragglers as they came down to breakfast, and Logan watched her good humor. He thought she was charming.

After breakfast Kim began to make cookies. There was nothing to do all day. There was no opportunity to be alone with Logan, so she cooked and baked. She did batches of various kinds of cookies and froze a good many for lunches. For dinner she planned roast beef with all its traditional side dishes, except she substituted Yorkshire pudding for the potatoes, and she made pumpkin pies.

But for lunch that day she made a big pot of chili, served over a bed of rice and beans, with cheeses and crisp rolls; then she gave them ice cream and cookies for dessert.

All that day the lodge was filled with the scents of spices and the mouth-watering aromas of good things to eat. The men made sly forays into the kitchen to steal cookies, while she protested they would ruin their appetites. Because Logan was always near her, he heard as Bill said softly that his appetite wouldn't be satisfied with just cookies.

Apparently not understanding Bill, Kim replied, "There'll be pie after dinner."

The men were comfortable together. They spoke of many things, for they were all executives in large corporations, and there is a network of acquaintances among such men. Jennings and Bill were there together, discussing some deal. Jennings was the seller, but Bill was very casual about it. While they were all there for business purposes, they were all serious fishermen. Fishing was special to them, and they enjoyed it.

On that stormy day, they went over their hand-tied lures and discussed the merits of what kind to use for which fish. They tied more with great imagination. Kimberly was invited to view the proudly shown, tiny works of art; and there were some that were weird! She asked, "Now, what fish in its right mind would try to eat that?"

"See? We glean out the odd ones and make a stronger fish population. That gives us more sport, as the smarter ones are more difficult to catch. We have to work harder, be more clever, because who wants to be dumber than a fish?''

Although they regretted the lake was so rough, they weren't restless. It was a pleasant day of relaxation for them all. Well, not all. There were two tense men. Bill . . . and Logan, who was watching Bill.

Kimberly seemed unaware that Bill was trying to entice her. Logan didn't think any woman could possibly be that oblivious to a dangerously flirting man. Of course, she had only sisters, and her stepfather was a professor at Knox and everyone knows professors are vague and out of touch, but Kimberly was twenty-one years old! She ought to be more in tune than she appeared.

Logan made sure he didn't seem to watch Bill, who was sprawled on a chair in the kitchen and whose eyes never left Kim as he made light, teasing conversation. Kim laughed. Logan figured Bill had to be forty. He had a sureness about him that showed he was familiar with women. He looked as if he'd been around the block a time or two. He looked like a man who always got his way.

Bill ignored Logan as if he wasn't anywhere around. Logan was insulted to be so easily dismissed by another man. He was jealous. Jealous? My God, he was *jealous*! He couldn't be. It was just that instinctive male competitiveness. Kim was the only young woman around. She was attractive, and they were idle, so they wanted her attention. Bill wanted something more than just attention.

Couldn't Kim see that? There was nothing worse than a silly woman blundering right into some man's trap. Logan had seen it done before. Once or twice he'd been tempted to try it, but he'd always been concerned for the woman. He'd never seduced an unaware woman. He'd always been sure she knew exactly what she was doing. What was coming off? His mind went plowing along as he listened to Bill's risqué conversation.

Bill liked double meanings. He teased Kim with innuendos, but she went for the straight meaning every time. Bill loved it.

Logan wondered if Bill assumed she was teasing him back. Was she really that naive? God, he hoped not.

She wasn't. Bill was older than most of the men who ordinarily flirted with her. She didn't have much experience with mature men. Most of those she knew were married and unpracticed in the verbal teasing Bill used so skillfully. It required a quick wit to reply in such a vein, to keep it flirting and not descend into salaciousness.

The light tiptoeing around the edges of really naughty exchanges would be fun, but Bill wasn't teasing as a mental exercise. The exercise he had in mind was another kind entirely. He was using the conversation to pinpoint her degree of willingness. But she was too smart to follow his bait, so she bit her lip to keep from laughing, for he was very clever with his words, and she replied innocently.

"I understand you were hot before your dip in the lake. Are you cold now?" He was deliberately becoming more blatant.

"It's always a surprise when the weather changes so much in summer. Of course, it really isn't summer up here yet, in spite of it being June."

"I know of many ways to make you warm and cozy."

"It's warm enough in the kitchen. Being busy keeps anyone warm."

"I could keep you busy."

Logan interrupted with restrained heat, "You might find something else to do besides annoy the cook."

"Do I bother you?" Bill turned an indolent stare to Logan. For a sighted man, his question would be insulting, but Logan's angry eyes were off to the side.

Kim suggested mildly, "Perhaps you two should go out to the shed and chop some wood for the fireplace." She removed a tray of baked cookies, then slid another tray into the oven.

With faintly disguised disdain, Bill reminded Kim, "Logan can't see to chop wood. You've made enough cookies today to feed an army. How about quitting and coming out to the shed with me? You could admire me as I work hard to entertain you."

"Mr. Jennings is going to teach me to tie a fly."

Bill scoffed, "He wouldn't appreciate you. I'll show you how to find flies."

Logan said dangerously, "She's not going anywhere with you."

Not even looking at Logan, Bill asked Kim, "He your keeper?"

She smiled benignly. "My father appointed him over twenty years ago. I have to obey Logan."

"He's no protection for you; I'll take care of you."

Logan gave a sharp intake of breath, betraying his escalating anger, but Kim said mildly to Bill, as if there were no tension, "You must have led an interesting life." She had subtly emphasized his age.

"Leading," Bill corrected her. "Present tense."

Kim nodded but asked, "You have children?"

"I have a daughter."

"Then you're married?"

"Divorced. I'm free." He shifted impatiently in his chair.

"Aw. How awful it must be, to reach your age and to be alone." She gave him a sad look.

Logan listened, astonished. Kim knew what she was doing! With firm calculation, she was putting Bill's years into focus in order to widen the gap between them.

Had Bill behaved, she would never have done that image blurring to the older man, but he'd become too blatant. So she asked, "How old is your daughter?" Whatever he replied, she was prepared to be close to her age.

But he said, "I've always liked redheads. Are you a natural one?"

"I didn't get the freckles my father had. What's the color of your daughter's hair?"

"Why don't you wash out the rest of that gook? I'd like to see your hair as it should be. I'll bet it's beautiful."

Kim lifted her eyes from the dough she was forming into figure eights and gave Bill a big smile. "You sound just like my dad! *He* calls it that! You fathers must all be alike." She went on with her work.

Cautiously, Logan began to relax.

"What do you intend doing when you finish your business master's?" Bill was watching her differently now. His manner wasn't one of lazy indulgence. He was pursuing her a little grimly.

"I'll probably go to work. However, I might go on and get an additional degree, one in communications. That's the field of the future."

"When that time comes, get in touch with me. I have connections, and perhaps I could get you into something that would interest you."

"That would be years from now."

"I'll remember you."

Logan moved his head—slightly more alert—in response to the hazard in Bill's words to Kim. Not in the actual words but in the tone. Bill would remember Kim. To some women that might be a charming promise, but to someone like Kim, it could mean that whatever Bill had in mind would only benefit him. He would use her. She might get what she wanted in a position, but the position he had in mind wasn't a job.

Logan knew Kim had done her best to make Bill understand that she was not interested, but he didn't want to understand. It was the place, the enforced idleness due to the weather, but Bill couldn't give it up. He had no other distraction, and he was a restless man. He could well force a confrontation.

* * *

Again that night, Kim read to the eight men. Again they clamored for one more chapter, arguing that they weren't tired; it wasn't bedtime, and besides, they'd been inside all day and they weren't sleepy. They were hilarious. She laughed until tears came. They were clever men, and their arguments lent ideas to one another, so their campaign was built and honed until it was marvelous to hear. They enjoyed the nonsense and laughed at themselves as much as she did.

So she read two more chapters. But she stopped in order to keep the last two chapters for the next night. Bill called her Scheherazade. He made her quitting before the end of the book seem like a sexual teasing. She ignored him and his insinuation as she pleaded a hoarse voice, whispering, clowning, treating the men with the casual good humor she would use with her own father.

Although he seldom let his gaze rest exactly on her, Logan watched her hungrily. His ears took her voice into his head as his nose now knew her scent. He craved the taste and touch of her.

When she rose to go upstairs, and said her goodnights, Logan got up to escort her. Bill stood and Logan tensed, but Jennings said, "Bill, I have another idea. Let's see what you think of it."

"Tomorrow."

"How about now?" Jennings asked easily. "You're not going to bed yet, are you?"

Bill's gaze followed the pair heading for the stairs, Kim guiding Logan. Bill put his hands in his trouser pockets and said impatiently, "Okay. Let's go into the kitchen."

In the upper hall, Logan asked Kim, "Will you wash the color out of your hair? Or does it have to grow out?"

"No, there's a solution that takes it out easily enough."

"Will you?" He'd backed her against the wall by her door and pinned her there with his body.

She allowed it. She smiled up at him, and he appeared to look at her quite earnestly. Did he worry about her? "I can't wash it out. Not now. I'll leave it as it is. If I washed it out now, Bill would think I did it for him."

"Ahh." Logan's sigh was one of relief. "I wasn't sure you weren't attracted to him." He paused for a brief mental debate before he told her, "He's after you."

"He's just restless." She discounted the danger.

"So am I."

"Someone will come up the steps, and they'll get the impression you're bothering me."

"It's you who're bothering me, and speaking of impressions, I'd love to impress you." He pressed against her as he kissed her. All day he'd longed to do just that. He was wild to be alone with her.

While she kissed him with eagerness, she was still fully aware of where they were and of her particular situation. She was one woman with strange men, one of whom she liked and another who had signaled too clearly that he wanted her. Bill could be unpredictable. He could become very difficult, given the right circumstances. Like coming up the stairs and seeing her kissing Logan. She couldn't guess what he might do, and she didn't want to jeopardize Logan's safety... or her own.

So she squirmed and breathed, "We must not. Someone might come upstairs."

"Come to my room."

"I'm not that crazy."

"I'll take care of you." His breath was hot and his hands hard, the heels of his palms pressed into the sides of her breasts.

"Behave and there won't be any *reason* to have to take care of me."

Reluctantly Logan released her. All his muscles were tensed. "Lock your door. Don't open it to anyone."

She smiled tenderly. "Not even you."

"For me, you could open up." She reached up and ruffled his hair. He didn't move. He was thrilled she'd treat him so familiarly. She'd been almost as distant with him as she had with Bill. No soft glances, no touches. Nothing. But she had kissed him back.

He stood in the hall until she'd showered and was in her pajamas. Then he checked her room carefully and told her again to lock her door.

"Shall I move the dresser over in front of it, too?" She grinned at him.

"If anything happened, if he could get in, you'd yell for me, wouldn't you?"

"I'd scream the house down."

"Be careful." He kissed her.

"You're a little hyper."

"I've never been like this before." The fact surprised him as the realization sank into his consciousness. He kissed her again.

"It's because you don't have sisters and therefore you don't realize women can take care of themselves."

"A lot of rape victims would debate that." He kissed her another time.

"The great majority of rapes are done by 'friends' and relatives. Women sometimes hesitate to object soon enough and protect themselves diligently."

"Could you be diligent?"

"Very."

He wrapped his arms around her tightly and kissed her until she almost swooned. He lifted his mouth. "You didn't object."

"No." She had trouble forming the word.

"I could just toss you on the bed and take you." She smiled, and her pupils dilated. He groaned, holding her tightly, and put his head down by hers and hugged her hard to him. "I'm probably going to go berserk."

"No. You just need more exercise."

"All right. I know a good one that would help."

"You're as bad as Bill."

"No, I'm much, *much* better."

She laughed. "See? That's just what he would say. Do men have dictionaries of risqué conversation and word meanings?"

"In kindergarten it begins with Dick and Jane seeing each other."

"I'm not surprised. Let me go. If Bill saw us, he would assume I'm available. You must be discreet."

It was unarguable. He released her again, backed away, put his hands into his trouser pockets and turned toward his room...as Bill quietly came up the stairs. Kim had already stepped back into her room, and she simply closed the door...and locked it.

As she slid the bolt silently, solidly home, Bill tapped on the panel, causing her to jerk. "Kim?" His voice was low and husky.

"Good night."

"Open the door a minute," he coaxed in his deep voice.

"No. Good night."

"Kim?" He still tried.

Then Jennings's voice came along the hall. "Can I help you, Bill? Need a blanket? Ask Yollie."

"Never mind."

Kim lifted the covers and slid quietly into bed. It was very cold. She wished she had a hot-water bottle, but she wasn't going to open her door again. She pulled on socks and went back into bed. As she warmed, her mind became occupied with the difficulty represented by Bill's interest.

This was getting complicated. It could turn very touchy. Apparently Mr. Jennings was keeping an eye on the situation. When she'd come up to bed he'd kept Bill downstairs, and he'd come up the stairs right after Bill. But Jennings was trying to sell Bill something. How far would he go to help Kim if it meant jeopardizing the sale?

What she really should do was go home. As unfair as it was, it was still the woman who must avoid difficult situations. In ordinary circumstances, leaving would be the solution. But the terms of the legacy were that they had to stay there for two weeks. The others would leave on Sunday. They would fly out. The hulk who had flown her up was scheduled to come for them. Three days.

Three days more of walking on eggshells before the rest of them would all leave. Then there would be just Yollie, Jeb, Logan and she. Really it would be just Logan and she. Just the two of them. For five days? Or were others scheduled to come in? If there were, maybe there'd be some women this weekend. That would make it immeasurably easier.

The next morning, Jeb and Yollie were already in the kitchen when Kim came down. The wind was blustery and the lake was too rough for fishing, but, Jeb told her, several people were due in that very day, if the lake calmed down. He was to radio the conditions of the lake to Harry before noon. Then Jeb inquired of her, "You still want to be cook? We'll have a full house for a couple of days. They's just coming for the weekend."

"Any women?"

"Yep. A couple."

"Oh, good." Then, as she began the preparations for the day's meals, Kim asked, "What will they do today, with the lake so rough?"

Jeb replied, "Without the rain, the men'll be outside. There's pitch and catch, a basketball hoop for any lively ones, golf clubs and plastic practice balls, and there's always wood. City men think it's manly to chop wood." He shook his head. "Then there's my old truck motor that needs some loving care. It's always a challenge to some men."

"Why the truck? Where would you drive out here?"

Yollie began to reply, but he was all but unintelligible, so Jeb told her, "When we cut wood for the lodge and the outbuildings, we cut them in a winding track, 'round and 'bout. Good for hunting. And that way we can go out a ways and get wood with the truck without clearing too close to the lodge. People that come here don't particularly want open meadows."

"Clever." Kim was impressed.

"So're you," Jeb told her solemnly. "If I was fifty years younger, I'd give Bill and Logan a run for their money. You want to watch that Bill. He could be a handful. You're a good woman, a nice one, and it's been a pleasure. I worrit some when you got here. I thought you might be trouble."

"We're even. I thought you might be stupid." She raised her brows and gave him an aloof look, with a small, smug smile.

Jeb laughed, and Yollie howled in glee.

Logan rushed in. He looked around, jerking his head. He had instantly seen that Kim was relaxed and all right, but he had to pretend he needed assurance. "Kim? You okay?" He looked where she wasn't.

"Over here. I'm fine. Jeb just told me that when I got off the plane, he thought I might be trouble."

"Well, I can understand that." Logan took the cup of coffee from her hands, and an electric thrill went through him at that casual touch of her. He kept his eyes on the cup until he could breathe again.

Jeb and Yollie looked at the two and understood what was happening to them better than they did. The eccentric old men gave each other a communicating look and smiled, quite pleased.

Five

___

The wind had died by the middle of the morning. The world was clean, calm, and the lake began to settle down. By midafternoon it, too, was smooth enough and the new guests were flown in. Again the hulking pilot, Harry, had to disembark with the passengers in order to check up on the weirdo he'd brought in the week before and to see the reactions to the new bunch. His last week's report had entertained his wife.

Harry saw the girl's hair wasn't as wild. It would look okay, but it was still the same three colors. When he was closer, he saw the thin line of her red roots and figured she'd deliberately done that as accent marks to the rest of the mess.

Harry noticed the goggle-eyed man was without his glasses. Nice-looking guy but probably blind as a bat. The guy was standing by the girl and appeared to watch her, with only quick looks toward the new arrivals, who were two women in their mid-thirties and two older men.

Kim could see the women were dressed in new, expensive, beautifully designed outdoor garments. They looked like a posh magazine's advertising for a new line of athletic clothing. The men wore the usual serious fishermen outfits of comfortable flannel and jeans. They were distantly courteous to the women.

Kim thought the two women might just as well wear tags that said "We Are Exploring All the Places Where Men Are Supposed to Be Found." To meet men, women have to go where men go, so the two had come to this fishing "resort." The problem was, if they did meet some man, fall in love and marry, more than likely they would never go fishing again. These two women didn't have the look of fisherwomen. They had the look of cocktails and lace.

The men who came to such lodges might be power men with money, but when they had the time, they fished. With other men it might be football or hunting or cars or whatever it was that took them to those places where women found them.

Even Kim knew it wasn't the man a woman should seek out but an activity that interested *her*. Then she'd find not only a man but one who shared an interest. It was really only basic logic.

So, Kim thought, here were two "left thumbs" at this fishing lodge, and these hunting women would find Bill and Ned. Good. They were the right age for Bill. They'd distract him from her. Excellent. Kim smiled and waved a welcome.

The women gave a weak wave in return. They weren't there to become buddies with another woman. They eyed Logan as they came to the porch, followed by the new men and the pilot. The women saw that Logan was almost ten years younger than they. Then the scrawny Jeb hustled down the track toward them, and the women's faces became grim.

Kim could readily see the "resort" title had misled them, too. She almost called out that the plumbing was indoors, knowing that would give them a little heart.

Like Jennings, Morris and Patrick, the new men were in their fifties and married. The women were Julia and Tate. Tate, a brunette, was the stronger. She was aggressive, a hunter. Julia had been dragged along for company, conversation and bait. Blond and pretty, she was a pleasant, warm body who smiled a meaningless smile at everyone.

The women didn't share a room, and they were only barely mollified to find the indoor plumbing. They asked Kim, "Any other guests?"

"The two who will interest you are out fishing. There are three older married men, but then there're Bill and Ned."

Tate shot a look across at Logan. "How old?"

"Late thirties or early forties. Both divorced."

The sun came out.

Tate asked, "What do you do around here?"

Kim told them about Yollie's hibernation in the shed, her taking up the cooking and reading a book aloud while the men played hearts.

"Cards? *Reading?*" Tate inquired as if she hadn't heard right. "You're kidding me."

"You two should liven things up considerably." Kim grinned. They were open, unpretentious women. She liked them both. But she was honest enough to admit to herself that she was relieved the two were older. "I'm glad you're here."

"Leave it to us."

While the two women settled in, Kim said to Logan, "That solves Bill."

"I hope." He looked unconvinced. He thought even with her hair that way, Kim was far beyond either of the other two women.

Kim figured he was worried the women would latch on to him. "You're too young for them." She couldn't stop chuckles. Logan was superior to any man. Had Jennings been twenty years younger, he might have briefly distracted her, but as it was, Logan was the only man there. "You're safe," she assured him. "They already told me you're too young."

"Thank God for that."

So. He didn't want to be caught? He was just dallying with her. He sure acted like an interested man. If he was attracted, he only wanted an affair. Why should that hurt? She wasn't looking for a serious relationship, either. An affair with Logan wouldn't be feasible, since they lived three-quarters of the continent apart. With her at Knox in Galesburg and Logan clear out in Sacramento, they'd never see each other after this next week.

It was just as well. Her life was planned out perfectly. She really didn't want any distraction. But—

perhaps—she could do as Molly had suggested and have that brief, discreet affair?

However, when the women came back downstairs, in marvelous lounge clothes that were feminine and flattering, Kim felt a sharp sense of competition. They were so confident. Then the nagging thought sank into Kimberly that there were a lot of older-women, younger-men pairings. Was Logan really safe?

Kim had fixed a roast turkey to slice for sandwiches, but the fish weren't biting that day, so she served the turkey for dinner. The table conversation was lively, with much laughter. The women were clever, glib and funny. Everyone enjoyed them, including Kim.

Kim saw that Bill smiled as he lounged back idly in his chair, and he watched almost silently. She realized he was used to being pursued. The two women would have their work cut out for them to ensnare him.

Tate had Bill spotted for herself and left Ned to Julia. Logan didn't relax. He wasn't fooled. Bill wasn't distracted. However, Tate was very good at enticement. Not too blatant, not too rough, there was nothing coarse about her, and her humor was marvelous. She suggested dancing and supplied a player and tapes, some lively ones first and then slow dances.

The women danced with all the men. Tate cleverly chose Mr. Jennings first, and then she went easily around until it very naturally became Bill's turn to dance with her. She did it nicely. She was neither pushy nor greedy.

Tate was an excellent dancer, and she made the act a pleasure. But she did "accidentally" brush against

Bill. She did indicate she was interested. He ignored her overtures, but not rudely; he acted as if he hadn't noticed!

Logan danced with Kim, and they went well together. He'd known they would in every way. He held her gently in his arms, very conscious of her tender, soft body against him, but he about died of jealousy, because he knew the time would come when Bill would dance with her. Logan wanted to snatch her up and run off with her before that happened.

To distract herself from the fact that her body was against Logan's, Kim was watching Jennings and Morris dance together. They danced as men who like dancing will do when there aren't enough women to go around. They were so funny. Kim saw that Ned and Julia danced, already deep in conversation, ignoring everyone else. Jeb and Yollie watched. The other men played gin rummy. Then Bill asked Kim to dance.

She'd known that would probably happen, but as the music began, she felt a shiver inside her that was different from the delicious shiver Logan made in her body. She said, "Next time."

"You've danced with Logan. Dance with me." He took her hand and pulled her resisting body up from the chair and trapped her in his arms.

There was nothing Logan could do. Bill couldn't harm Kim, with all those other people there, so he had to allow it as long as Bill didn't embarrass Kim in any way. He watched them like a clever hawk with faulty vision.

"Have you given Logan any reason to be so possessive?" Bill was holding Kim forcefully against him, opposing her tensed muscles, which tried for space between them.

"You're holding me too tightly."

"Not nearly close enough." His voice was low and husky.

"I can't dance this way. Let go."

"Just relax and enjoy it," he coaxed.

"I can't breathe."

So he slid his hand down to the small of her back and clasped it tightly there. That allowed her to lean back, but then she gave him a curt look. "Let go."

With the hand that held hers he indicated Tate, who was dancing with Patrick. "Why can't you be that friendly to me?"

"I'm too young."

But instead of putting him off, she made him laugh. When the piece was over, Bill didn't release her and waited for the next dance, but Jennings said, "I haven't had my dance with Kimberly. My turn." And he simply took Kim's hand and smiled at Bill, who released her very, very slowly.

Kim wondered if Jennings had just blown his sale.

It was Jeb who solved the partners shuffle. He had been housing guests for fifty years, and he could sense controversy a mile away. He poked Yollie, and they began to clamor for the last two chapters of the book Kim had been reading.

She protested, "But the new arrivals haven't heard the first part. It isn't fair to them."

Yollie volunteered, "I tel'm." But when he took a breath to begin a synopsis, Jennings took over and gave a concise recounting of the essence of the plot, with excited little sidelines from various others. Tate laughed and responded so marvelously that it was to her they told it all.

Then Kim read the last two chapters to avid listeners. Some of them gathered around her, lounging on the floor. Tate, Julia, Ned and Logan were among those on the floor. Tate mentioned there were thirteen in the room, then she rendered a dramatic story of the thirteenth guest's mysterious murder.

Kim chaffed Tate, "Thanks just a whole lot for such a lurid bedtime story. When I was coming up here to meet Logan, as our fathers had arranged, my sisters said that in the trackless woods in the wilds of Canada, Logan would undoubtedly turn into a chain saw murderer. And now you bring up the murder of the thirteenth guest!"

That brought protests from Logan, but there was agreement from everyone else: "He *looks* like one!"

Julia said, "Murderers are always smoldering and darkly handsome so you never suspect them."

"No," countered Patrick. "I suspected him from the day he arrived."

And Jennings agreed. "It wouldn't surprise me one bit."

Then Logan laughed. "With my sight, I'd probably attack trees."

Tate asked gently, "What happened to your sight?"

"My eyes have been just this way since birth." As always, he was totally honest.

"That must have been tough." Tate reached out and smoothed his eyebrow with one finger.

Tate's gesture startled Logan, but it shocked Kim. Tate had said he was too young. No one did that sort of thing to any young man over five. A woman only did something like that to a man she was dead set on attracting! Tate hadn't done anything so personal to Bill. Why Logan? Kim became quite hostile and protective. As she was a redhead, her cheeks flushed and her emerald eyes flashed.

Seeing this, Logan was delighted.

As the guests moved around, some hungry and searching out the cookie jar or a sandwich, Bill spoke to Tate. She nodded, then spoke to Logan, who called to Kim, "How about a walk?"

"Great." Kim was pleased he'd singled her out, and she got a sweater to go outside.

But as she went out the door, Tate came along. "We'll go, too." And she and Bill came out onto the porch.

Now how was Kim to back out? She didn't want Tate out in the dark with Logan. Logan took her hand, and they left the porch together. But as soon as they were on the trail, Tate said, "Let me," as she came between Kim and Logan with practiced ease, separated the pair, took Logan's hand and moved away.

Logan stopped to explain to Tate his protection of Kim, but Bill had taken Kim's arm and pulled her aside.

Kim drew in a breath to tell Bill to back off, but just then something Tate said made Logan laugh. The laugh was so sharing that it hit a nerve in Kim, and she allowed Bill to move her away from the other two. She heard Logan's cautioning "Kim," and she slowed, but she walked with Bill.

Bill behaved perfectly. He wasn't as careless with his hands as Logan, but then he could see better. Kim peeked back to see how Logan was behaving with Tate, and it was impressive to Kim that she didn't burst a blood vessel. Tate wasn't leading him along by the hand as she was supposed to. She was walking arm in arm and pressing against his side!

"Lose something?" Bill asked with laughter running through his words.

"No." She flung back her red-rooted green-black-and-gold hair.

"You look exotic."

"I borrowed my sixteen-year-old sister's clothes and hair color. She's orange, green and yellow."

"Why did you dye your hair that way?"

Since that was a logical question, Kim replied, "To discourage the chain saw murderer."

Bill laughed with real amusement. "But there was the chance such a combination would set off a precariously balanced psyche."

"We didn't consider that."

"You sure as hell set me off," he confided huskily.

"You've been in the woods too long if the natives are beginning to look good."

"I'd like to see you out of those lumpy sweaters."

"I have to admit they're formfitting." She was mimicking her sister's responses as closely as she could imagine the way Pat would reply.

"I'm from Chicago. That's not too far from Galesburg."

"It's a lot farther than you would ever believe."

"You could come up for a weekend. I could show you a lot of things."

"Bill, you're about the same age my father would have been if he'd survived Nam."

"He was a very young father. I'm not an old man."

"That's true. What I'm trying to say is that while that is true, I'm very young. I wasn't young at eighteen, but now that I'm twenty-one, I've become quite astonished how much I don't know."

"I could teach you."

"After a couple of months, you would long for someone who could communicate with you."

"I don't need a communicator. I want a warm companion who charms me."

"Obviously you had one. What happened?"

"We lost the link. I became involved in my business. I'm a very successful man, but that takes a lot of time. My daughter was sent to boarding schools, and my wife became bored. There was nothing to fill her time. She began to run around, so I divorced her. She's with her fifth lover, the girl's still in boarding school, and I'm a lonely man. Money isn't enough. I want to begin again. I'd be very careful of you. You could have anything you wanted."

"I have what I want: I'm in school. I'll finish. I have plans, but they don't necessarily include a man."

"Any man? Or just not me?"

"You're almost twenty years older than I. If I ever do marry, it won't be for years yet. I have the time, and then I'd want a husband who would be around when the kids need him. I don't want to own the

world. I just want a nice, ordinary life with the freedom to travel, to investigate, to contribute." They
were stopped on the trail; their exchange had so en-
grossed them that neither had noticed that Tate and
Logan were standing, listening.

Tate said, "Brava!" But she said it softly. "Here's
Kim," she said to Logan. Then she explained to Kim,
"He believes you're the only one who knows how to
lead him through the paths. He may be right." She
smiled up at Logan and relinquished him, then she
said to Bill, "So, how's the stock market doing today?"

Bill laughed. "How did you know?"

"You're of a type. I happen to be genuinely interested. I've just bought some stock in..." And they
strolled off in the night light.

Logan said, "How did you get along? Were you
okay?"

"He's lonely."

"I can't believe he would use that line." Logan was
disgusted.

"I think he really is. If he just knew it, Tate is perfect for him."

"You're a matchmaker?"

"No," Kim declared. "I'm clear-eyed, nonroman-
tic, levelheaded, practical and logical."

"That's frightening."

"Damn. I should have used that on Bill. Instead, I
was honest."

"Then you're not levelheaded and logical?"

"And practical—you forgot that. I am. In aces. But I told him why I couldn't come to Chicago to see him or—"

"He asked you to *Chicago*?"

"What's the matter?" Kim inquired.

"Why...the bastard!"

"Asking me to Chicago makes him a bastard? I've been asked to St. Louis and Indianapolis and Cincinnati. Were they all bastards, too?"

"Probably. Did you go?" He glared at her.

"Of course not! Don't be silly. Can't you just see me saying to my mother and father, 'Bill Sawyer asked me to Chicago for an illicit weekend'? All *hell* would break loose in a very gentle shock that I could never withstand."

"Ah, the gentle shock. It's effective. Haven't they ever yelled at you? I've found myself straining against the violent urge to yell at you, and I've only known you for a week."

"Has a week gone already? I wondered how these two long, endless weeks would ever drag past. I was so glad Yollie had locked himself in the shed. Cooking gave us something to do."

"Would you come out to California?"

"You need a cook?"

"I need you."

"Now, how could you possibly know that? We're strangers."

He agreed with her. "You *are* strange, but I'm perfectly normal. Come out to California. We can get you transferred out there to finish up your last year. We have good schools."

Look what we've got for you:

... A FREE compact umbrella
... plus a sampler set of 4 terrific
Silhouette Desire® novels,
specially selected by our editors.

... PLUS a surprise mystery gift
that will delight you.

All this just for trying our preview service!

With your trial, you'll get SNEAK PREVIEWS
to 6 new Silhouette Desire® novels a month—
before they're available in stores—with 10% off
retail on any books you keep (just $2.24 each)—
and FREE home delivery besides.

Plus There's More!

You'll also get our newsletter, packed with news of your
favorite authors and upcoming books—FREE! And as a
valued reader, we'll be sending you additional free gifts
from time to time—as a token of our appreciation.

THERE IS NO CATCH. You're not required to buy a single book ever. You may cancel preview service privileges
anytime, if you want. The free gifts are yours anyway. It's
a super-sweet deal if ever there was one. Try us and see!

Get 4 FREE full-length Silhouette Desire® novels.

Plus
a handy
compact
umbrella

Plus
a surprise
free gift

▼ PLUS LOTS MORE! MAIL THIS CARD TODAY ▼

Silhouette's Best-Ever "Get Acquainted" Offer

Yes, I'll try the Silhouette preview service under the terms outlined on the opposite page. Send me 4 free Silhouette Desire® novels, a free compact umbrella and a free mystery gift.

225 CIL JAYE

PLACE STICKER
FOR 6 FREE GIFTS
HERE

NAME _____

ADDRESS _____ APT. _____

CITY _____

STATE _____ ZIP CODE _____

Gift offer limited to new subscribers, one per household. Terms and prices subject to change.

PRINTED IN U.S.A.

Don't forget...

...Return this card today to receive your 4 free books, free compact umbrella and free mystery gift.

...You will receive books before they're available in stores and at a discount off retail prices.

...No obligation. Keep only the books you want and cancel anytime.

If offer card is missing, write to: Silhouette Books, 901 Fuhrmann Blvd., P.O. Box 1867, Buffalo, NY 14269-1867

"But California is going to break—"

"Don't you *dare* to say that. We're all tired of hearing it. Texas would love it—they'd make blue jokes about it—but when Californians are reminded of it, they take it seriously."

"Texas isn't going to slide into the Pacific."

"It'd be like them to cut themselves off and float out into the gulf just for the lark. Did you hear about their navy?"

"No."

"If we had sleeping bags, we could go out into the woods and spend the night."

"What's that have to do with the Texas navy?"

"I realized I was wasting time talking about something I'm not really interested in."

"Wait till Texas hears *that*!"

"What I'm interested in is getting you into a sleeping bag," he clarified.

"Although this place doesn't qualify as a town, I suspect this is very similar to some other invitations I've received, and I just wonder if my father's good friend Mac had a bastard for a son."

"I suppose that's possible, but I'm sure...you mean me?"

"There was that very suspicious invitation you just gave me concerning sleeping bags."

"You think plotting the heavenly bodies is salacious? For shame!"

"You only mentioned sleeping bags. You didn't mention charting the stars."

"I *supposed* since we were talking about the Lone *Star* State, you would understand my drift of thought."

"Oh. Of course. Sorry."

"I should think so. Women are a very strange race of humans. You resist integrating. A melding of races would advance the country."

"Are you implying that if I crawl into a sleeping bag with you, I'll be helping my country?"

"Of course!" He expressed great astonishment. "Why else?"

"And here I thought you were just interested in hanky-panky. I had no idea you were trying to help our country."

"So you admit I'm not the bastardly type who would lure you into a sleeping bag for carnal purposes."

"Not you." Kim smiled at him.

"Well . . . I could be convinced."

"Now you're trying to get me to coax you? How very wily you are, Logan Pederson. Do you know you spell your name wrong? Anyone in Galesburg will tell you it should be spelled with a *T*."

"Tederson?" He was amazed.

"No, you idiot. P-e-*t*-e-r-s-o-n."

"I suppose there was an ancestor who wanted to be different and wasn't smart enough to just dye her hair three colors, so she changed the spelling of her name."

"If she was Scandinavian, her name would have been Petersdauter. A boy would have to've been the one to change it to Pederson."

"Then it was *he* who wanted to dye his hair all those colors. And since dye was so chancy in those olden days, he changed his name. And we've had to spell it, correct people's pronunciations and be wrongly labeled ever since."

"Living's tough," she said in false sympathy, but then she remembered how poor his eyes were, and she took his arm and hugged it to her chest in compassion.

Wasn't she aware how soft her body was to his arm? He stopped and kissed her. He held her body hungrily to his, and his heated mouth sought hers. His big hot hands held her, then moved tensely on her body, holding her close. He slid his arms around her, tightening those bonds, as he deepened the kiss.

Kim was startled by the flood of longing that surged through her. She stood up on tiptoe and recklessly wound her arms around his shoulders with her hands in his dark silken hair. And she matched the greed of his kiss, trying to squirm closer to him.

They were all alone, they thought, out there in the woods, but Tate and Bill saw them, and coming up the path, Ned and Julia did, too.

Six

To be caught kissing wasn't too bad, but the kiss being exchanged by Logan and Kim was so hot that its passion touched the watchers like a burning shock. The interrupted pair didn't leap apart; they had been stunned by the kiss, and they parted slowly, almost in a trance. Kim's arms slid down Logan's broad chest, through his big hands, and he caught her trailing hands and held them, not wanting to let her go.

Tate said, "Excuse us. We didn't mean to intrude." The words were gentle. They could have been snide, but Tate was really a very nice woman. She knew Kim was embarrassed, or would be when she surfaced. Right now Kim was quite blank. As Tate and Bill passed the pair, Bill hesitated, reluctant to leave Kim. But Tate said, "Shall we?" and joined Ned and Julia to return to the lodge, and Bill did follow.

The pair watched the foursome disappear down the trail. Logan told Kim, "I didn't mean to get so out of hand, but you affect me wildly. I want to carry you off."

"That doesn't sound like the son of a liberated woman."

"That makes it all the worse. I thought I really was a staunch advocate of feminism. How can I explain this strange possessiveness I feel for you? I'd have you locked away, in transparent trousers and a veil and wearing bells all the time."

"Hold it!"

"Somehow I knew you'd hesitate."

"Hesitate? That's adamant opposition!"

"Let's get the sleeping bags and discuss the advantages of female slavery."

"I can remember my mother's shock when the Shah was overthrown in Iran. Not that she was pro-Shah, but in two weeks, the women were out of school and back in the veil. *Two weeks!* We don't realize how fragile our rights are. All of us. All of our rights. We need to pay attention."

"I . . . really wasn't talking about other women. I believe Tate and Julia are perfectly free to do whatever they want, along with every other woman in the world. It's just you who affect me in this way."

"Are you a member of an underground men's group that's using devious ways to lure women out of liberation? Are you a recruiter for the overthrow of NOW? Is this some clever campaign to blind me to what's going on?"

"Welll..." he began reluctantly, then pretended candor: "I didn't realize you were that smart. We thought it might work. Since there're more of you than us, we're each supposed to be responsible for two women. Our next step is harems. Want to be first girl?"

"*First* girl?"

"Another stumbling block?"

"I don't even want a divorced man. Why would I want to share a man?"

"That shows disruptive, selfish tendencies. We'll need to work on you."

"Let me guess. The sleeping bags again?"

"Bag. Singular. I just made it plural until I could get you out there in the woods."

"You fight sly."

"We must. Women have gotten completely out of hand. They aren't just independent acting; they *are* independent. They do everything! They have all kinds of clever gadgets to open jars and to reach things, and they've almost eliminated zippers and back buttons. With sperm banks, they're making us redundant."

"Donors are still needed for the sperm banks."

"Big deal. That's like having someone else eat your dessert or take your aspirin. Or scratch your itches. Or..."

Kim guessed sagely, "You've been talking to horse breeders who can't have an equestrian sperm bank."

"Ah, yes. Thoroughbreds must do their own breeding so that one stallion isn't the sire of all racehorses. Soon horses could have it better than men do."

"Do you suppose it's being in the woods, in this rather primitive location, that's set you off?"

"We could explore that possibility. It's the environment-over-heredity syndrome. Either that or Mac wasn't the easy man Mother always said he was. Do you suppose she's misled me in order to influence me?"

"Never. Women fight fair."

"Well, I always thought so, but how can I explain the way I feel about you?"

Kim smiled. "She never remarried."

"So I've inherited loyalty. You think I'm hooked on you?"

"No, no, no. Just that when you're attracted, you take it seriously."

"Don't you?" he asked. "You kiss seriously."

"I've never been kissed that way before. You scramble my brain cells."

"Hah! It *works*! We'll have the women back where they belong in no time! Chained to the kitchen stove, barefoot and pregnant!"

"Good grief!"

"You thought I was just fooling around, lured in by your three-colored hair—four, actually, if you count the red roots—but all this is an international conspiracy. 'Get the redhead—she'll be disguised, but she's the key to the future of the Women's Movement. Get her and we can stop it cold.'" He grinned at her in the moonlight, seemingly looking right at her, and he said, "Scrambled, huh. I must be getting pretty good. Let's see if I can do it again, so I can be sure it wasn't a fluke."

"I don't believe . . ."

He soothed her. "In the interests of research."

"Oh . . ."

So her mouth was just right, with that word, and he applied himself with great concentration, diligence and enthusiasm. He enjoyed his work. He was careful, he was gentle, he coaxed her into intense cooperation. And it worked again.

Her head swooned as the cells joyfully rescrambled themselves, and that had to be the reason all her nerve endings vibrated and danced with such sinuous glee. They set off quivers of exciting sensations throughout the whole network of cells that made up her body, with throbbings of sensuality in secret places. It was all astonishing.

But while her body became softened and malleable, his shivered with his restraint, and his cells and muscles and nerves tensed into rigidity. His hands were hard, his arms were bands, his feet were planted, his body was a wall of muscle against which hers melted and adjusted, squirming closer.

He lifted his mouth only a fraction with the thrilling little myriad sounds of their lips parting. His breath scorched as he growled low and quietly, "I give up. Women rule."

With each slow word a sigh, and using soft lips that touched his, she replied, "No challenge at all."

"Not right now, at any rate. Lead me down the primrose path."

She laughed the delicious laugh of a woman who is being teased by a man she likes very, very well.

"Kim!"

It was Bill calling.

"Don't answer," Logan urged.

"If I don't, he'll come looking."

"We'll go off down the track. Let him look."

"I'm a little cool for a night in the woods."

"I'll keep you warm," he promised salaciously.

"My feet freeze."

"Women are such a quagmire of problems. I'm amazed men put up with them."

"They do it all the time, and deliberately!" She laughed.

He loosened his arms. "The sleeping bag?"

She shook her head.

In a strong voice Bill called, "Kim!"

He was closer. Kim pushed her hands against Logan's chest. "Let go. I don't want him to see us like this."

"Why not? You think he'll be jealous? Are you trying to make him jealous?"

"No. I'm trying to make him think I'm too young to be fooling around."

"He saw us kiss once."

"Let go."

"Kim!"

"Here," she called negligently, and took Logan's hand as if they'd been returning from a long walk. Logan could hardly put one foot in front of the other.

"There you are. I brought you a sweater. It's getting cold."

"We were just coming in."

"Are you all right?" He looked at Logan as if his arrival had prevented Logan from murdering Kimberly.

Logan said in a lazy voice, "She's with me."

Bill nudged his criticism, "That's what worried me."

Kim assured Bill, "There was no need to worry. I was with Logan. You know he can't see well."

"It wasn't his seeing that worried me," Bill ground out through his teeth.

And Logan had the audacity to laugh.

Bill didn't take the laughter at all well—it seemed to set his teeth on edge—and the three returned to the darkened lodge in a pithy silence. They went up the stairs, where Bill stood, leaning his back against the wall with his arms folded. He stayed just that way, in the upstairs hall, until Kim had brushed her teeth and gone to the door of her room.

As silently as Bill, Logan had stood by Kim's door until she said good-night, then he leaned down for a brief kiss. She gave him a cautioning look, went in and locked her door. Through the door she heard the two men exchange a snapped word or two, then their footsteps going in opposite directions. She sighed and went to bed and slept.

Four-thirty came much too early. Kim wanted to stretch and just lie in bed and reflect on all that was happening. But she rolled out and went to the bathroom for a quick shower. She dressed again—or still—in Pat's clothes and went into the hall as Logan came from his room. She waited, smiling, and he came to her to kiss her sweetly. Then he patted her bottom as she turned away.

How had Logan known she was in the hall? She hadn't said anything. He'd come from his room and smiled at her. Had he seen the light from her door? It must have been that.

Tate was in the kitchen, drinking coffee. She'd made the pot. She and Kim smiled at each other. They were silent as Kim brought out the rolls and loaves from the cooler and set them to rise. Then she got out the ham slices for breakfast, mixed the batter, set out the eggs and got organized. She began to slice yesterday's chilled bread for sandwiches for lunch. It wasn't until then that Tate felt she wouldn't distract Kim from her planning. "Bill has some very strong feelings for you. Give me Logan. At least the weekend wouldn't be wasted."

Kim stopped and stared.

Tate went on. "I heard you on the trail. Your thinking is excellent. You could become a force in the women's world. As yet you're a nubilous woman, still unformed, but when you get out into the business world, you could become a part of a strong network. Bill would be good for you. He could teach you a lot. But if you go along with Logan, you'll end up a little wife and mother, and you'll be wasted. Stop this interlude with Logan before it goes too far, and pay attention to Bill. He's a man with clout. I only wish he was attracted to me."

Kim shook her head. "He isn't really attracted to me. He's only bored and competitive. He's too old for me, or I'm much too young for him. He's an impressive man. If I were your age, I'd find a way to catch his attention, but I'm not sure I want any man.''

''Then you're leading Logan astray. You have him tied in knots.''

''You know why we're here?''

''Yes, it's a charming story. Your fathers planned this. How interesting. Ah! So that's why you dyed your hair?''

''You should have seen it moussed!''

Tate laughed. ''A disguise?''

''As you can see by the roots, I'm a redhead. I've found some men get strange around redheaded woman. Why, I have no idea. So my sisters and I decided I'd look . . . different. My younger sister Pat has her hair in orange, yellow and green, and I'm wearing her clothes.''

''They said you came with green lipstick and nails and painted your cheeks gold?''

Kim nodded. ''At home, we had a great time doing it. I thought it would turn off anyone. I'm surprised both Logan and Bill aren't leery of me. Look at my clothes!''

''When he first saw you, you must have rocked Logan.''

''He had on a bow tie with his flannel shirt, and he'd parted his hair in the middle and slicked it down. That was before he broke his glasses. He's practically blind, you know, and he looked like a country owl.''

''Oh?'' Tate looked thoughtful.

But just then the country owl came into the kitchen. He was without the glasses, his hair was in the perfect tumble of an expensive haircut, and he wasn't wearing the bow tie. Tate smiled as she understood. Ah, yes. What was sauce for the goose was sauce for the gander.

Logan's glance swept the room. Tate was conscious when his sharp glance slid over her, and she smiled wider. He'd seen and dismissed her. Yes, she thought, this was one hell of a weekend. Two good men had weighed her up and found her lacking. She looked at Kimberly. What did Kim have that she didn't? Besīdes being fifteen years younger, Kim *was* a redhead. That was salve for Tate's wounded pride. Who could compete with a natural redhead?

Logan did an excellent job of searching a way across the kitchen to the coffee, where he "found" Kim, who greeted him. "Tate's here."

Then Tate was sure. Logan could see perfectly well. But she went along. "Good morning, Logan. Sorry. I should have spoken, but I forgot you can't see." She did try, but she couldn't quite keep the drollness from her words.

"G'morning." Logan knew Tate had him figured out! How had he betrayed himself? How did she know? *Would she tell Kim?*

"Coffee?" Kim asked him.

"Please." Logan was waiting for Tate to expose his sham. How would Kim take it? And he found it wasn't a joke. He'd fooled her, but she wasn't someone he wanted to trick. He would have to find a way to tell her so that she wouldn't hit the ceiling. She'd be furious. So he was silent. His replies to their chatting were brief.

Kim leaned down and looked into his face. "Are you all right?"

She touched his cheek so sweetly that he ached down into his guilty conscience. "I'm fine."

Tate watched them rather fondly. She'd just met them yesterday and already felt she knew them. Strange. They were really darling. But they made her think of another time, another life, and she became pensive. The only solution was to get busy. "May I do the sandwiches, or is there a method to it?"

"A serious method. You slap everything available between two slices of bread."

"Ah, how clever. May I apprentice?"

"Well, the list is full for apprenticeship, but I'll accept you if you are willing to pay the price for a slot."

"What's that?"

Kim's bantering words became serious. "Keep Bill away from me."

"I will try, but it would be better if you set me a more plausible goal."

"I believe your 'try' is another's win."

"I love flattery. You do realize my ego is bruised enough for one weekend?"

"I doubt you know what ego is."

"I wish you were older. I would love to have you for a friend."

"What's age?"

Making her words sound deliberate, Tate told Kim, "I believe, if you would take the course I suggested, we could become friends with much in common, but I'm pretty sure you will ignore my brilliant advice and go your own way."

"I'll let you know."

Logan put in, "You women are talking over my head, and I find I'm very curious as to what the hell it's about?"

Kim patted his cheek in a condescending manner and said, "You're too young."

In that wink of an eye, what with one thing and another, Logan had had *enough*. He swooped Kim around, flipped her over his knee and lifted one big hand to swat her. But he couldn't do it. As he hesitated, Kim struggled free of Logan's loosened grasp and stood up. She was red faced, with emerald-sparked eyes. Logan watched her, almost as mad.

Kimberly snapped at Logan, "Just why did you do that?"

"Sassiness."

"You *are* too young!"

"Not for you, I'm not!"

Tate was pleased that Logan couldn't bring himself to actually swat Kim. Dividing the ingredients for the sandwiches, she glanced at the two glaring furiously at each other.

But Bill walked in, just as Kim put her hands on her hips and took a deep breath to say something excessively telling to Logan. Logan sat and waited, but Kim looked up at Bill and didn't say anything.

Bill asked, "Need some help? What's going on? What did he say? Why are you angry?"

"It's nothing." Kim turned around in a snit.

Bill came over to Kim and took hold of her arm.

...and like a slowly uncoiling steel spring, a very dangerous Logan stood up.

Tate paused, sobered.

Bill asked Kim, "If it's nothing, why are you so angry?"

Kim jerked her arm from Bill's fingers and snarled, "Because I'm redheaded, and being redheaded allows me to show my temper anytime I want to—like now! Now, leave me alone!"

Bill drew his head back a couple of inches as if she'd slapped him. His lips parted in surprise and he stared. Then he frowned at Logan, who watched him narrow eyed as if trying to see him. Finally Bill looked to Tate, who was fascinated. He asked her, "What the hell's going on?"

"Have some coffee."

Bill stood for a minute, then he moved rather stiffly, as if he might need to counter a blow of some kind, and he poured himself a cup of coffee. There was a dead silence. The two men were both on their feet; the two women worked at the preparation of the meals.

"Fish biting today?" Tate asked pleasantly.

Bill glanced at her and saw Tate wasn't at all interested in any reply; it was an open, tension-breaking question. "Probably." He saw that for some reason Tate was amused.

She asked, "What will you catch today?"

"Pike."

The others drifted in. They got their cups of coffee, and Kim began the eggs and pancakes. The conversation eddied around the three silent ones. With that same strange amusement, Tate replied for the other three so that they appeared to be normal. It entertained Tate. She said, "Since I'm here, I would like to fish. I intend to catch more than anyone else, and I'll put twenty cents on it.''

They each cheerfully put up the required twenty cents, and the cash was put in a bowl on the table with the names of the bettors. Tate matched all the bets. Jeb outfitted Tate with pole and instructions, and she went with Jeb's group. With so many fishing, four boats went out. Tate was not in Bill's boat. She gave him no indication that she even knew he existed.

Four stayed in the lodge. Julia and Ned, still upstairs...and Logan and Kim. Logan said to Kim, "I'm sorry I handled you so roughly."

"Part of your back-to-nature?" Kim snapped.

"You asked for it."

"A typical male reply for anything he does that's violent. I asked for it. Like rape. The woman demands rape. She's a woman, so she should expect it."

"You're way around the bend from an almost swat. Why'd you act that way? I asked what you two were talking about because I had the feeling you were deciding something about us, and I wanted to know what the hell you were up to. I want a part of any decision you make about us. I had the strong suspicion that you might try to slip away from me."

She looked at him in amazement. "It was nothing like that. Tate wanted a chance at you, and I wouldn't let her." That wasn't exactly right, but Logan was basically the reason for the conversation.

Logan smiled. His eyes closed almost halfway. "Why wouldn't you let her have me?"

"Exactly what I said: you're too young."

He moved, watching his feet for a minute, then he commented mildly, "I understand older women can be quite an experience. Interesting. Different. Easier." He drew out the last word.

"She said I could learn a lot from Bill."

"No!"

Kim raised her eyebrows. "Why 'interesting' for you with an older woman but 'no' for me with an older man? Is this discrimination? Prejudice? For shame!"

"Don't get sassy."

"Because I'll risk being swatted?"

"I doubt I'd ever try to give you another."

"Another?" Her tone held a warning.

"Man, but you get mad! Do you fly off the handle like that often?"

"I did not say one word! What do you mean, I flew off the handle? I was perfectly calm."

"Your multicolored hair stood on end and your eyes shot sparks! It's a wonder I didn't burn to a crisp!"

She watched him. "How do you know my hair stood on end?"

"Did it? I felt it. I felt as if an electrical charge had zapped me." He was talking rather fast. "I never realized a time would come when I'd welcome Bill walking into a room. That's a strong lesson for us all. A time could come when we could welcome an enemy. Another marvel of living."

She laughed.

"I'm forgiven?" he asked.

"I suppose."

"I could never hurt you."

He went to her and took her into his arms. He kissed her first. He'd had only one kiss, and he was starved for more. He held her, hugged her and kissed her in a lovely way. Then he held her to him, groaning as he nuzzled his face against the side of her throat. He took her earlobe into his mouth. He pretended to gnaw at her shoulder. His breath steamed as he nudged aside her sweater and rubbed his teeth gently on her shoulder.

He had her trapped against the counter and was down to some serious gnawing, when Ned and Julia came sleepily into the kitchen. They smiled rather dewy smiles, and Kim suddenly realized they'd spent the night together. They'd just *met*! And... How shocking!

Ned and Julia were very casual about being together. Not the least awkward. They laughed and touched and acted as if everyone behaved in such a manner. They had no need for Logan or Kim; in fact, they ignored the younger couple, took their breakfasts out onto the porch and ate there, sitting close together, talking, laughing.

"That's what you wanted me to do," Kim accused.

"We're nothing like that, and you know it."

"A couple of days more getting acquainted? Is that the difference?"

"I'd have taken you on the dock that first day," Logan declared.

"Do you mean to tell me you were attracted to such a weird woman as I was when I landed?"

"Honey, you're still weird. A week here hasn't changed you a bit. Your nails are pink again, and you've given up the green lipstick. Your face is scrubbed, and your hair lies naturally, but it's still all those colors, and your clothes are just the same.''

"If I looked normal, you wouldn't be interested?''

"After Bill leaves tomorrow, you can come out of your disguise and I'll see. It'll be a crucial test. Don't be nervous. I'll be kind.''

"Why. . . you *beast*!'' Kim huffed.

"I thought you wanted honesty!''

"Even if I did wash my hair, how would you be able to see it?'' She watched him intently. Did he hesitate?

"That's the actual test. I don't need to see you to know you. You've been betraying yourself all along as a superior woman. I am taken with you.'' He made it his declaration.

"Taken?''

"Attracted?''

"I'm the sole person around here who is anywhere near your age. That's the attraction. Since I'm the only one younger than you, you can feel superior to me. Feel is the crucial word. No one is superior to me.'' She gave a thought or two, then added, "A couple might be equal, but none superior.''

"I could become accustomed to you.''

"We'll have to arrange to meet after you get your glasses replaced, so you can see the real me.''

"You'll have the summer off. With the money from our fathers, you won't have to work. Come to California. I have a job. But you could stay with me. I'd—''

"Stay with you?''

"You know. In my apartment.''

"Why would I do that?" she asked in surprise.

"To save money."

She watched him for a minute. "What would save me?"

"I would."

"From you?" She smiled a little.

"From yourself. You need me."

She laughed.

"You're not taking this seriously. You're in danger."

"Really? From what?"

"Other men. I have to save you from losing yourself to another man."

Seven

───

While Logan ran the dishwasher, scrubbed the tables and counters and swept the floor, Kim made her preparations for dinner. She again made pies. With four more people to feed, it took that much more time. An additional pie, a larger cake, another loaf of bread, more breakfast rolls.

Logan emptied the dishwasher, set the table for dinner and washed the pots and pans Kim had finished using. They worked well together. He knew what to do, anticipated what she needed and handled it all. He was a big help.

He swept out the common room and dusted. Swept off the porch and steps. Then came back to Kim and watched her. She gave him a sassy look with a grin. "You've done a great job. Have a cookie."

"Okay. Come on."

"I?"

"You're the cook, cooks are called cookie—I'll take you. Let's go."

"I believe you're getting too much sleep."

"That can't be true. I toss and turn all night long. I've had to remake my bed from scratch every morning—it's torn apart somehow during the night. I've been unable to sleep since you got off that plane and stood there like a psychedelic poster, held out your hand and said, 'We have crazy fathers in common.' I knew then that I had to have you."

"What was so great about saying that? They were crazy!"

"For you to stand there looking like that and accuse someone else of being crazy?"

"I only *looked* that way. I'm perfectly logical, levelheaded and practical."

"But with a redhead's temper."

"Only when some idiot turns me over his knee and threatens to swat me."

"You don't get mad about anything else?"

"Of course not."

"Are we going to go on a picnic today and soak the lines to entertain the fish?"

"Sure. Why not?"

"I'll get things ready."

"I saved some shrimp from last night's hors d'oeuvres for bait."

"You took *sea* shrimp from our plates to tempt freshwater fish?"

"One does as one must. I decided the reason we haven't caught any fish is that they're bored with the bait they've been getting from the regular bunch. The fish in this lake are gourmands. I'll pander to their taste buds.''

''How about mine?''

''Any particular thing you'd like for lunch?''

''A cookie.''

Not paying any attention to his earlier definition of cookie, she added a double handful to their basket as Ned and Julia came wandering in. ''Picnic?''

Disappointed to be interrupted, Kim was reluctant with her words. ''We are trying to snare a fish in the classic, bent-pin manner. We've been unsuccessful so far. Would you two like to come along?''

Surfeited for the time being, the new lovers raised eyebrows to each other and asked, ''Okay?'' and allowed themselves to be convinced with no other word from Kim—or Logan. He hadn't echoed Kim's invitation and was irritated by it.

Kim added more of everything to the basket, and Ned added wine. They carried sleeping bags along, and Kim guided Logan's steps. With the others along, now was not the time for him to tell Kim he could see perfectly well.

Ned and Julia were cheerful companions, but they weren't energetic. After they ate, they carried their sleeping bag off a way into some trees and out of sight. Logan grinned and Kim raised her eyebrows, and she firmly resisted Logan's lovemaking. ''What if they came back?''

''They won't. Let me love you.''

''No. Not now. Stop it!'' she hissed.

But he was exuberant over the "not now" and had to kiss her a time or two. She allowed it—she even kissed him back—but she didn't melt, because she was too self-conscious. Finally the two of them stretched out on the other bag and actually napped. Since they'd been getting up so early, they were tired enough and they did sleep.

The fish wakened Logan. He sat up. "We've got a fish!" Then he remembered to say, "I can hear it! Quick, Kim, grab the pole!"

She gasped, then scrambled witlessly and ran to the pole. Logan followed her, yelling. Kim grabbed the pole and jerked it out of the water. And a glorious trout came up from the water in an arc, let go of the pin and dropped back in a gorgeous splash almost in slow motion. *It got away!* she shrieked. "Grab it!" She flung the pole aside and leaped into the water.

"Kim!" Logan reached to stop her.

"What's wrong?" Ned and Julia came running.

"The fish!" Kim was splashing and reaching around in the water.

"She catches them with her bare hands?" Ned was amazed. "Isn't the water rather cold, to do it that way?"

"I'll bet she could do anything." Julia was admiring.

"Let it go!" Logan shouted. "Kim, get back up here!"

"I've got it! Stop! Quit wiggling! Damn! I've *got* it!" And she stood up with the wiggling fish clutched against her chest. The fish was enormous. Her eyes were, too. She hugged the fish tightly and moved her feet with care. "Don't touch me. I might drop it. My God! It's gigantic!"

The three were at the edge of the water, not knowing how to help; they were tensed and exclaiming, as their hands twitched in body English, trying to help. Ned and Logan waded the several feet out to Kim. Ned said, "Don't let go."

"I won't."

Ned took control. "I'll just put my fingers through the gills. Logan, grasp it just above the tail. Keep hold, Kim. Don't let go."

"I won't," she said again, very earnestly.

The three walked, testing each step, until they were on the bank and ten feet back from the water; then they all leaned over and put the trout on the ground before they whooped and danced and shouted and laughed. They'd caught a fish!

Logan scolded, "Get out of those clothes. You'll freeze! Here, take my shirt."

"Here's my sweater." Ned peeled it off.

Kim's teeth were chattering, but she didn't want to leave the fish.

Julia promised, "I'll guard it with my life."

Kim ran into the trees and tried to unbutton with shaking, cold fingers. She was still laughing excitedly.

"I'll get a bucket," Logan said, and turned toward the trail.

"No! You'll take forever," Julia objected. "I'll go."

But Kim yelled, "No! Julia! You're guarding the fish with your life!"

"I'll go!" Ned said, and he ran all the way back for a tub.

Kim emerged with Ned's sweater tied around her hips and wearing Logan's shirt. Logan then put his sweater around her shoulders. She grinned up at him. "I got it."

"What a determined woman you are!" Logan laughed.

When Ned returned, they filled the tub with lake water and put the fish in it, and they all stood around admiring Kim's catch. It was a monster.

Kim suggested, "If we let it go, we can say it was ten feet long."

Ned and Logan exclaimed simultaneously, as if they'd practiced it, "Let it go?"

"The fish that got away." She was laughing, still excited.

Following Kim and Julia, who carried all the rest of their stuff, Logan and Ned carried the tub. They got to the lodge and put the tubbed fish on the porch. Kim changed out of her sweater-shirt outfit, which had looked perfectly normal with her hair. The men changed jeans before they got another bottle of wine to drink a toast to the fish.

Julia helped put the finishing touches on dinner. Since that day's catch would be iced to be taken back home with the guests, the meal would have ham with canned sweet potatoes, green beans, applesauce. There were biscuits, strawberry jam and, for dessert, the pies. Then with anticipatory smiles and laughter, the four waited for the fisherpeople to return.

When the boats approached, the two couples went down on the dock and stood waving. They admired the exhibited catch with smiles and congratulations, then walked with the weary ones up to the porch.

Finally someone remembered to ask the daily question, "You guys get anything with your bent pins?"

Logan replied, "Kim did."

They were all courteous about a fish caught with a bent pin, then the four indicated the tub and showed off the fish. The first several viewers gave the tub a glance and exclaimed, then the others crowded around. There were whoops and shouts and much laughter. Kim's fish won the day's pot for the largest fish.

There were unsorted questions and comments.

"What'd you use?"

"You got that monster just offshore?"

"What'd you use for bait?"

"Shrimp," she said casually.

"Crawdads?"

"Sea shrimp." She covered a yawn.

"And you caught it on a bent *pin*?"

"She caught it bare-handed." Logan smiled.

Then they all told the story in a jumble. Logan began, "I heard it thrashing."

Ned added, "There was this god-awful screech!"

Kim explained, "It let go!"

"She went off the bank into the water." Logan was gesturing.

Kim put her arms around her body and said, "I about froze!"

Ned put in, "We all three held on."

And finally Julia got to say, "They came one step at a time, very slowly."

Then Logan added the ringer, "She wanted to throw it back and claim it was ten feet long."

Kim proved how logical she could be. "Well, you know, the one that got away."

"Let's have it for supper!" This was Jeb's idea.

"Elmer?" gasped Kim.

"You *named* it?" Bill was amazed.

But Tate helped. Quite firmly she said, "You can't eat something with a name."

Of course, in any sport there are the purists, like bent-pin advocates, but there were a couple of rod-and-reelers who questioned whether Kim's catching a fish bare-handed qualified her in the daily competition with those who used lures and hooks.

That led to a heated, hilarious debate. Fingers were likened to hooks. Kim was indignant. They were still arguing through dinner. And it was after that when Tate paid off her slew of debts to all but Bill. Bill hadn't made a bet. Tate had caught only one fish. It was her first of legal length, and she was going to have it stuffed and mounted. Jeb couldn't believe it. She was firm.

So Jeb packed the little fish in ice, then gave Tate the name of a taxidermist who... might mount it.

How queer it was, Jeb thought as he listened and watched his guests, how such different people could get to be such good friends in just a couple of days. Some groups stayed like strange dogs for the entire time. Stiff with one another. Nice enough but staying apart. This bunch was one of the special groups, and each one was a part of the whole. At such times Jeb felt almost as if it was wrong to take their money, he enjoyed them so much, but he stifled such notions and managed to collect his fees.

Getting Kim and Logan together was interesting. Of course, he and Yollie—and Jennings—had known the girl's father.

Jennings had decided they shouldn't tell the kids they'd known Gus. He'd said they couldn't "...uhhh, contribute to the situation," but they could watch. It was better if the kids thought they were strangers. That way they would be easier, more natural.

Gus had been a lot like his daughter. Open. A friend. He did his share. It was nice to see her here with that boy. Both good-looking. Kim was a surprise, because Gus hadn't been at all pretty. But his daughter was a beauty, and Logan was a fine young man.

Would it work? They seemed to take to each other. For a while there he'd thought Bill might put a monkey wrench into the spokes, but Kim hadn't been interested. He and Jennings had been uneasy when Bill wouldn't quit. Jennings had helped Kim with that. Actually, Bill might have helped with the two kids...he'd made Logan possessive.

Jeb felt it was for sure that Logan was hooked. He might not know it yet, but he was. What about Kim? Well, they'd just see if they couldn't give the situation a little extra nudge.

Jeb came out of his mental soliloquy to listen to his guests. This was their last night. They stayed up later. No one played cards or read. Their conversations went on very noisily, with a lot of laughter. It was nice, listening to it. And he watched Logan and Kim.

It wasn't until then that Jeb had the leisure to watch, and he understood that Logan could see. The laughter bubbled in him, and he looked at Jennings to see if he knew. If he did, he wasn't letting on about it. While Jeb didn't laugh out loud, he couldn't erase his big grin. People were so entertaining. Eventually they all parted, except for Ned and Julia, and went to their beds. It had been a great weekend.

Lying in his separate bed, Logan thought that he never had any real time with Kim. She worked in the kitchen with such dedication. Then there was always someone underfoot, blundering in, interrupting. He was with Kim constantly, but he had to keep his hands to himself.

He wanted to touch her. He wanted more than that, but he also just wanted to touch her. To put a finger on her cheek. To smooth her eyebrow. To feel the satin of her lips. To tickle her ear. He was aware of her every gesture, every expression, every movement. He longed for her. He wanted to sit and openly watch her. His peripheral vision was a godsend. How would he have survived if he'd truly had such poor sight?

His nights drove him mad with the memory of her sporting naked in the frigid waters of the lake. She was perfect. Her wild, colorful hair, and that red triangle, which betrayed the true color of her decorations. The slim beauty of her body, with its marvels of roundness. Her long, slender legs, her hands so graceful. And her laugh.

Her humor. Her sassiness. Her tart replies. She was so gentle. She was so special. And *he* hadn't wanted to come there. What if he hadn't? What if he'd allowed Dan to come in his place and Dan had met her first? The very thought of Dan kissing her was almost worse than the thought of Bill doing it.

And in her own room, Kim was equally frustrated. She had fooled herself into thinking this was the time for the discreet affair. And yet, there was no opportunity! How had Julia signaled Ned? They had met and gone to bed together in less than six hours—smoothly done, with no problems. Maybe if Logan could see better, there might be something in an exchanged look?

When they had been naked to go into the water and he'd touched her breast, she'd assumed it was by accident. The feel of his touch had flickered through her body like lightning. Maybe that had been her opportunity to indicate that she was willing to explore... well, to...uh...to try it.

He never really looked at her. She would glance up, expecting to see him trying to see her, but he was never looking in her direction. He was such a good companion, and he worked hard, doing more than his share. He had a nice disposition, and he was simply breathtaking. His body was superbly put together. So interesting. So well made. He... Maybe he didn't want anything more than a light flirtation? His kisses were mind-bending. Perhaps he didn't realize to what extent he affected her?

Kim understood that really talented people seldom realize others don't have their ability, like artists or musicians or people who know words and can communicate. With Logan, Kim's "vocabulary" was very limited. How did one go about initiating an affair? She went to sleep plotting.

Since it was the last day of that weekend, Kim hauled herself out of bed at four-thirty again and began the meal preparations. Logan came down, a little tousled and looking fabulous. She smiled at him, and he came straight to her. She was aware of how well he moved through the room and was pleased he was learning to avoid the kitchen hazards quite well. He took her into his arms and kissed her so hungrily that she knew it wasn't all talent. He really wanted more.

She laughed breathlessly and pried him loose. "I really have to get organized." But she was mostly admonishing herself, because she looked around the kitchen with her hands to her head, and it was as if she'd never seen the place before that moment.

It was at breakfast that Jeb said, "Yollie and me'll be going into town. Yollie's due a holiday, and I have business to tend to."

The guests all knew that would leave Logan and Kim there alone.

Jeb saw that while Logan accepted the news with no outward sign, Kim's eyes widened, but she made no protest. Bill's body jerked. For some reason, that bothered Jeb more than an outright objection. Then Jeb worried that Bill would stay over. And he knew if Bill stayed, he would stay.

How interesting it was to Jeb that he was now willing to lay down his life for that little girl with her four-colored hair. Why would he do that? His gaze rested on her and he smiled. She was busily eating and keeping track of the serving plates that might need refilling. As Jeb watched, she licked a dollop of syrup from the corner of her mouth, unaware how seductive she was, but Jeb noted that Logan saw it. So did Bill. She was just a natural-born woman. She'd be a treasure for any man. Jeb wished he were fifty years younger and sighed. Then his smile came back. He'd still be himself, and competing with Logan? What a farce!

But the thing about Kim was that it wouldn't be the covering of the man that would attract her. It would be the inner man. If she'd been a calculating woman, she'd have taken Bill.

Logan, too, measured Bill's bulk and weighed his chances. If Bill stayed—and Bill was beginning to make noises in that direction—maybe he and Kim should just leave with the rest of the group. The money from their fathers wasn't worth any risk to Kim. There would be room in the larger plane for all but one. So if Bill did decide to stay, he could, and both Logan and Kim could leave.

As they tidied the kitchen after breakfast, Logan said as much to Kim. She studied him quietly. "You'd give up the legacy?"

"Of course."

"If you stayed, you should get half. I'd explain to the trustees."

"I go with you."

She smiled at him, and he came to her and kissed her. So they went upstairs and packed their things, just in case, and told Jeb what they'd decided.

Jeb nodded, and he smiled at the pair. They would do. Yes, they would. They'd sorted out what was important to them.

But before Bill's decision could be positively stated, Jennings growled quietly to Bill, "If you stay, the deal's off." And Bill looked into hard, glinting eyes, but he didn't reply.

Some of the party had decided to fish again that morning, and some wandered around. Tate had to try the track, and several of the men went with her and took guns because there was the chance of bears. Julia and Ned disappeared upstairs. And some of the guests tinkered with Jeb's truck. It was a lazy morning, easy and friendly.

Just before noon, when the plane landed, the departing group was all packed and ready. Tate and Julia, in city clothes and heels, looked like Birds of Paradise.

Tate, too, had been concerned for Kim, so when Bill turned up on the dock, ready to go, she was so pleased Bill had been sensible that she briefly took his arm. Bill looked at her unseeing, wound up tighter than a top. So Tate mentioned that to Jennings. Jennings shrugged and said, "If we all leave together, that will solve everything."

Bill told Kim, "I'll be in touch," and he boarded along with all the rest. Kim didn't reply. The line was taken in, the motors roared, and the plane taxied out. Logan and Kim waved as the plane skimmed over the lake to take off into the wind, and they were alone. Just them. Nobody else was anywhere around. They were isolated in the middle of a wilderness.

To immediately take her into the empty lodge and up to his room seemed a little crass even to Logan. So he suggested nicely that perhaps they should go out to their cove with their lunch, as they had just about every day.

Kim had wondered what they would do. She felt painfully awkward and was having trouble keeping her greedy hands off him. She didn't want to hurry them into a shuffling, awkward coupling. But going out to the cove sounded very nice and easy. So they went into the lodge and prepared their picnic lunch.

Except for yesterday with Ned and Julia, they'd always carried a blanket along. This time Logan took a sleeping bag. Kim gave it a serious look of deep anticipation. "It's softer," he explained. And she accepted that, but he added two bottles of wine to their lunch. And a gun. They were all by themselves.

Logan carried the basket and sleeping bag, while Kim walked beside him, warning him of roots and low-hanging limbs, which she held for him. She discovered he had become as familiar with the path as he was with the kitchen. She could tell he anticipated the hazards. Just from watching Logan, she understood how blind people could get around in a known area. Having stumbled over things enough times, he'd learned to avoid them.

They settled their things in their small cove. They set their lines before they had their lunch, out there by the lake in the woods, with no one else around. Logan asked, "Why fish? How can you compete with yesterday's catch?"

"We came 'fishing,' so it's only honest to give a token gesture to fishing."

"Shrimp again?"

"No. We didn't have any more." She wasn't using any bait. Who wanted to be interrupted again?

They had turkey with ham-and-cheese sandwiches, pickles of course, an apple each, cookies and the wine. They toasted their brilliant fathers, the day, the elegant lodge . . . and each other.

With no possibility of interruption, it was wonderfully peaceful. The air was crystalline, so pure their view was sharp and distinct. Well, Kim amended, hers was. "I wish you could see better. It's so clear that everything looks fake. Like an amazingly contrived hologram. It is marvelous."

"I would like to see you up close."

"How much do you actually see? There are times I believe you see quite well."

"Really?" Now was the time to tell her. "Kim . . ."

"Can you see me now?" On her hands and knees, she'd moved closer.

Now, what man would interrupt the potential of such a testing? "Closer would be better."

She crawled closer. "How about now?"

"Just a bit closer."

She came within two feet. "Is this close enough?"

He replied just as honestly as he'd always done, "Almost."

"If I came any closer, I'd be in your lap."

"Let's try it that way."

"I'm not sure about that. The last time I was on your lap, you almost swatted me!"

He reached out and effortlessly pulled her to him, lifting and turning her, arranging her as he wanted, with her across his lap, facing him. He smiled down at her.

"Can you see me *now*?" She laughed.

"You make my head swim."

"But can you see me?"

"Kimberly Miller, you are just beautiful."

"Well, that proves I have to get even closer." She braced her lower hand on the ground and put her other hand on his shoulder to lever herself up, and, with her breasts pressing against his chest, she put her nose to his.

"Now can you see me?"

Instead of replying, he kissed her.

When he lifted his mouth, she was quiet. He gazed down at her. "People who are unsighted can tell a lot by their fingertips." He lifted one hand and moved his fingers over her face. His touch was exquisite. "Kim," he began his confession.

"How blind are you?"

"There are other ways of being blind than not seeing."

"Is this our bit of philosophy for today?"

"And the rest is you must never believe all of what you hear and see."

"How enigmatic of you! Are you telling me something? Is it a warning? *Are* you a murderer? What shouldn't I believe?" She studied him in return. Then she said softly, "You can see." Her pupils widened and her lips parted in a smile. "You fraud! You can *see*! Well, if that isn't just the limit! You fake! Here

I've been, leading you around!'' And she laughed. She put her head back and laughed, then she hugged him and said, "I'm just so glad!"

She astounded him. Of all the reactions he'd anticipated, joy hadn't been one. She was simply glad for him.

Eight

You're not angry with me?" He'd caused her so much trouble, leading him around, he'd thought she'd at least be annoyed with him.

"You didn't dye your hair." Kim grinned.

"So. That's why you did it."

"Of course." She opened out her hands. "And you parted your hair in the middle, slicked it down and wore that stupid bow tie."

"There's nothing stupid about bow ties," he told her in mock indignation. "They're elegant with evening dress."

She shook her head. "Not with flannel plaid shirts."

"Jeb went to town wearing a tie with his flannel shirt, and he looked sharp."

"Now, you know full well that a solid-color tie with a sports jacket in town is one thing, but out here a bow tie is another thing entirely. With your cuffs buttoned.'' Her eyes danced with her teasing.

"So you knew I was a sham?"

"No. I honestly thought you were an innocent trying to look country."

That insulted him, but she only laughed. He looked down at her lying across his chest in his arms and he smiled back at her. "I love you."

"Do you?"

"I've played right into our fathers' hands and fallen in love with you just as they expected. How do you think they had such foresight? Do you love me, Kim?"

"Almost immediately. I felt sorry for you."

"Good Lord, sorry? That's awful!"

"No, I wanted to protect you."

"I'm not sure I like that."

"You looked so out of place that I worried you wouldn't fit in and be comfortable; then you couldn't see, you fraud. That was at first. But I quickly realized protecting you would be a waste of time, because you're not protectable."

"I'm not protectable? Is there such a word?"

"Of course there is—I just said it. You aren't protectable because you're a very serious protector."

"With you."

"Yes."

"So you've known I loved you?"

"Not the first day. I was still taking care of you. I knew you were attracted; I just didn't realize you loved me until you said you'd give up the money for me. That it wasn't important."

"Outside of something really criminal, I don't know of anything I wouldn't do for you. I am completely committed." Logan was very grave.

Kim was hedging. "I'm determined to go to graduate school. In this day and age, with all the problems there are in marriages, a woman is a fool not to be prepared to take care of herself."

"You won't need that. I'll take care of you."

"I suppose every man tells that to every woman he marries, but in ninety percent of the households in this country, women work."

"I haven't objected to your being prepared. I think it's the right thing to do. I have no problem with you getting an advanced degree. For all the trickery we've done with each other, we've come through this very well. I even love it that you were so afraid of me that you came disguised."

"So did you."

"Mother thinks I'm a good catch. She told me to be careful of you, that you might fall in love with me."

"Are you a good catch as an accountant? I accepted that you actually were one, with those thick glasses. The glasses go with my mental image of one."

"Mothers tend to be prejudiced."

"Figuring out how we work this is going to be a little difficult. We should wait to... Are you going to ask me to marry you, or is it too soon?"

"Will you marry me?"

She asked, "Did I make things awkward for you? Have you given that careful thought?"

"For some time."

"It could be just sex. Your kisses scramble my brain."

"No one else ever complained of that."

"How many women have you kissed?"

"Uh . . ."

"Well?"

"I'm trying to remember."

She chuckled. "You're a fraud through and through!"

"I'm not fraudulent about loving you. You're so special I'll probably build a monument to our fathers. What if I'd never met you?"

"Don't you think we would have found each other somehow?"

It thrilled him that she considered they had been fated to meet. As if she believed that of all the eligible—and acceptable—matches they could make, only they two were perfect. He kissed her, and it was the usual, devastatingly remarkable kiss. He lifted his mouth and looked at her intensely.

She opened crossed eyes and said, "Who or what are you? Where am I? What's happened?"

His voice husky, he explained, "I happened to you." Then he got down to serious communication. He moved her against him. His hands cupped and smoothed her body, his mouth savored hers, and she helped. They were soon gasping for air and making sounds of hunger . . .

. . . And there was a thrashing sound from the water! *They'd caught another bloody fish!*

They looked at each other in astonishment. She said, "How crude!"

"Intruding on us that way! No tact." The water churned. "Probably bigger than Elmer."

"He must really be caught on that pin. How barbaric. Let's let him go."

"To let him go, I have to release you, and I don't want to."

"I won't run off. I'll be right here."

"Never? Always?"

"Yes," she agreed.

"Forever."

"Deal." She grinned. How romantic. Yes. It was. "Logan, are you going to make love to me?"

"Yes."

"I'm not...you know...I'm not on the pill or anything."

"I have protection for you."

With his reply, she became a little indignant. "Do you mean to tell me that you brought protection along with you up here to the wilds of northern Canada? Did you just expect me to...well, you know?"

"No. I received a package in the mail from a friend of mine when the new people came the other day. A box of one hundred!" He burst out laughing. "We're going to have to really be diligent if we're to use this twenty-four hours well."

"A...hundred?"

"The spirit's willing," he told her with a shrug as he gave her a quizzical look and she laughed.

They released the fish and watched it swim away in a streak of colors. They exchanged a look of mutual satisfaction. They kissed very ardently, then, hand in hand, they went back to the sleeping bag, where he stopped her. Very slowly he took off her great, bulky sweater and bra, then her slacks and panties. He disrobed her as if he'd discovered a treasure beyond worth. He stepped back and just looked at her. She stood still in her wild hair, with her beautiful decorations, and allowed him to see her. But she blushed scarlet. Like the fish, she, too, was a rainbow of colors.

She became too self-conscious just standing there, so she went to him and lifted her fingers to his shirt buttons, but he didn't have the time. He skinned out of his things quickly in order to hold her. She had wanted to gaze at him, but he simply could not wait. He was a little awkward, too, and she was charmed by him.

He'd never been so conscious of the way he looked before. Why now? And he decided that before, it had been experimental, so he hadn't cared so much, but this was real. This was serious. This was forever.

Their kisses steamed as their tongues touched hotly. They explored each other, there in their Eden. Their hands were gentle and loving. Their murmurs were sweet and breathless. And she allowed him all the privileges she'd denied to every other man. They slowly moved down to the bag's soft surface. He worshiped her. He loved her. He built a fire in her that scorched, and she moved and sighed and murmured, pulling at him, lifting to him, allowing her body its instinctive need to entice. Her mouth to caress. Her hands to cherish.

But his need was raging. He moved more earnestly, his hands were harder, his mouth became demanding, and he tautened to iron. He leaned over her, filmed with a fevered sweat in that cool air, and he gulped air. "Kim." It wasn't a question. It was just that she was there, where he wanted her. Then he asked, "Now?"

She nodded in tiny, impatient jerks as she pulled at him. He lay on her, entered gently, then thrust. She curled, gasping, and made a sound that thrilled him passionately. She wanted him as badly! She was as thrilled as he!

He lay still, breathing raggedly, and she made soft, pleasured sounds as her hands moved on his head and shoulders and the soles of her feet moved on the backs of his legs. She was impatient, while he struggled for control. He leaned up on his elbows and put his head in his hands, trying to distract himself, but she kissed along his arms and slid her hands down the sides of them, and wiggled just a bit beneath him.

"Hold still," he said.

"Why?"

"I have to last longer than a rabbit. I'm a man. I want to please you. Hold still for just a minute, until I can go slower."

She said, "All right." But then her hands went to his sides, and she ran her fingernails lightly along his skin. It didn't help him. He goose-bumped *all* over, and he grinned down at her, the fires leaping in his eyes. He pressed into her. She moved her chest under his lifted chest. But her soft breasts were trapped and rolled against him.

"You're driving me crazy," he warned her.

"Do you want me to lie completely still?"

"For a minute."

She spread her arms and legs out in a large X, looked off into the sky and hummed, pretending indifference. He drew air in through his teeth, and she smiled up into his eyes. "Okay now?"

"I think this time is going to be very fast. I wish I could wait, but I'm just not sure I can forget where you are."

"Close your eyes. Then you won't see me."

He laughed and lay on her, his head in the cove of her neck and shoulder. "I love you."

"Not yet. You're delaying."

He moved a little.

"Ahh."

"You like that?"

"I believe I do."

He lifted his head in quick concern. "Are you okay?"

"Almost. Move a little more."

Watching her face, he did. Slowly. "How's that?"

"Better. A little harder."

Completely caught by her, he forgot himself, and he began to please just her. It was fantastic. In pleasuring her, he found exquisite pleasure himself. He loved her wildly, and she responded uninhibitedly. It was true loving. The giving of each to the other. Completely. Completed. For a while.

He moved them to one side and pulled the rest of the sleeping bag over them. They smiled and kissed. He hugged her. They held each other, and, relaxed, they slept in great contentment, all their hungers replete, all their frustrations solved. They knew and shared the love, and it would be forever.

It was about two-thirty that afternoon when they wakened. They hugged and yawned and stretched, very aware of each other, of their nakedness. "I've wanted you just like this ever since you got off that plane."

"You have a penchant for strange-looking females?"

"Just one."

"I'm not strange looking. I'm very ordinary. I just wanted to thwart any odd devotion caused by an anchorless male who wanted to share my half of the legacy, in addition to his own."

"I keep forgetting about the money. What will you do with yours?"

"Even sharing with my sisters—and I will—there will be enough to go on to graduate school. Dad's teaching there pays my undergrad fees. If there's any of the legacy left over, I'll set it aside for something special. How about the down payment on a house, or a sabbatical sometime? What do you think? Would you like a year off somewhere along our lives?"

"You mean to share it." It wasn't a question.

"Oh, yes."

"I thought I would do the same thing. Your schooling. Our lives."

"I was so grim about coming up here." She moved her fingers in his hair as they lay facing each other, their eyes locked.

He shared the knowledge: "It's a good thing we didn't know each other before. We'd have been married already."

"Do you suppose?"

"No question."

"I'm glad I was the only woman your age up here. If there'd been anyone else, I'd have had a tough time getting your attention. I believe my dad planned it exactly that way. No competition for me. Easy."

That intrigued him. "Uh, how would you go about getting my attention?"

"Oh, after I'd washed all the goop out of my hair, I'd wink." She winked. "And I'd smile." She smiled. "And I'd ask you to help me to do things, then I'd—"

"So that's why you volunteered to do the cooking! You just kept me around so you could work on me! I'm a victim! And all that time you kept saying thank God Yollie was locked in the shed so we had something to do to pass the time. You *planned* all this!"

She laughed and sputtered.

"Women are too crafty for us innocent men. I can't believe I was lured in by kitchen work! How will my sons ever hold up their heads? They'll say, 'How did you catch Momma?' And I'll hem and haw, and finally I'll say, 'I helped in the kitchen.' They'll think I submitted to a dominant feminist!"

"Your mother." His mother still worried her a little. She was a strong woman. There could be contention.

"Mother's had me out from under foot every chance she got. She loves me and she wishes me well, but *she* isn't the woman who snookered me into submission. She taught me to stand on my own two feet and howl. With you I'm no wolf—I'm a puppy dog.''

He sounded so amused that she had to grin, but then he raised himself up over her and looked down on her, daring her to deny he was submissive.

''Puppy dog,'' she snorted in disbelief.

He put out his tongue and panted. Then he leaned his head down and lapped with his heated, slow tongue across her sensitive breast. With his big hard hand he sought her stomach. He moved that hand to her breast, spread his fingers widely and rubbed his palm slowly over it. He curled his fingers and pushed with the heel of his hand as he kneaded her soft flesh. With his lips he took her nipple and suckled it deep into his hot mouth, tugging on it gently, his tongue stroking the underside marvelously.

She began to twitch in tiny movements, and her breathing became shallow. Her hands went to his head, and she held it tightly against her as his mouth worked leisurely on her breast. It was astonishing.

Slowly his fingers moved to search her out, then his hand went to her hip and turned her toward him and pulled her closer as he reached farther and touched her. It was like fire.

Her breathing began to labor, as if she were set to climb an impossible mountain but would never make it. She needed help. His. She gasped, and her hands moved. They caressed. And it was he who gasped and almost shuddered with her touch. He took her mouth in scalding kisses that lingered. Deepened. Then passion became urgent as need heightened, but this time they were less rushed. They could relish. They could tempt and tease. They could explore more fully, and did, each fascinated, each responding, each pleasing the other.

"I've heard," she said, and stopped.

"What?"

"Could I . . . ?" And again she stopped.

"Anything."

So she pushed against him, indicating he should lie flat, then she sat up to lean over him and did to him the things he'd been doing to her. He dug his fingers into the fabric of the sleeping bag under him, and it was his breathing that was labored, his teeth that clenched and his voice that groaned.

"Do you like that?" she'd ask.

"Yes."

"I do, too." And she'd do it again. Or she'd move her mouth and lick or suckle, and she'd ask, "Do you mind my doing that to you?"

His voice sounded strangled. "Not at all."

"I find it fascinating."

"Me, too," he would agree fervently.

She became quite bold, and she explored minutely while he shivered and stiffened to rigidity. Even that fascinated her. But he couldn't yet give such freedom only to her and not be a part of the exploration. His hands couldn't be still, and he had to kiss her. "Now kiss me." And she'd lift her head and kiss his mouth. His consumed hers. He moved his hands on her soft body, and they became feverish and needy. He put her down flat, took her, and they made love again. Exquisitely.

"How marvelous it is," she said sometime later. "What a lovely gift is love."

"Yes."

"Is it always like this?"

"This is very different."

"I've nothing to compare it to. Have you ever lived with a woman?"

"No."

"Have you ever been engaged?"

"No. I must have been waiting for you," he said gently.

"As I did for you."

"I know. I'm glad you did."

"I am, too." Her voice was tender.

"Kiss me."

"I find that's a very dangerous thing to do."

"You're safe right now."

She leaned and kissed him softly, then smiled into his eyes. "I need a bath."

"We could try the lake."

"That's too cold. I don't want to put on my clothes again, not without a bath. I'm very sticky."

"I'm not surprised. There's no one else around. We could just gather up our clothes and walk back to the lodge, take a shower together and go to bed. Right?"

She laughed delightfully and tousled his hair.

He cautioned, "That's an erotic thing for you to do."

"Oops, sorry." She jumped up from the sleeping bag and began to gather her clothes. "I prefer the warmth of a shower to the liquid ice of the lake."

"Now? Maybe next week." He curled on the sleeping bag and closed his eyes.

"If you go with me, I'll carry half; but if I go alone, I don't carry anything."

"See? I'm a slave."

"Naturally."

He opened his eyes, looked upon his naked love and smiled at her. "I'm up."

"I meant for you to get up."

"Of course." But he sat up and then stood, groaning over the effort. They gathered their gear and carried it all back to the lodge. Then they went up the stairs and showered together. Kim used the remover and washed out the tricolored goop. Logan watched, fascinated, and at last she matched.

Their shower took such a long, *long* time that they ran out of hot water. That was all that made them leave the shower stall. But by then Kim was meticulously bathed, and so was he—simply from having been under the water so long.

Kim blow-dried her hair and moussed it normally. She had never cared so much about how she looked. She wanted Logan to see her as she could be, so she then puffed her hair with her hands before she turned and displayed the finished product.

He was dazzled. "I thought you were beautiful before, but you're stunning." He was a little shocked.

She scoffed as she began to dress while he watched her. He thought she was amazing. She was real. She was all the things he ever wanted in a woman, and on top of that, she was really lovely.

When he told her yet again that she was beautiful, she said quite thumpingly, "Not only are you a fraud—and much too good-looking for anyone's good—but you have a glib tongue, and my mother has always warned us girls about men with glib tongues."

He stuck out his tongue, then said, "It's an ordinary, everyday tongue. Why would you think it...glib?"

"Glib-tongued men talk women into all kinds of things."

"Like...what?" he questioned glibly.

"Like picnic lunches on a lakeshore and carrying along sleeping bags to 'sit on' so they can use their talented tongues."

"I never realized redheaded women could be so logical and knowing. How did you figure out I was trying to have my wily way with you?"

"I was trying to help you," she replied quite logically.

"You could have mentioned that. It would have saved me a great deal of frustration."

"Were you frustrated?"

"Excruciatingly so."

"Tell me where it hurt."

So he did, and she sympathized so nicely, so tenderly. But she was laughing.

It was by then almost four o'clock. They dressed, and he began to move her things into his room. Naturally she asked, "Just what do you think you're doing?"

"That's a good example of being redundant. What's it look like?"

"You can't do that."

"Why do you say I can't do it, when you just asked what I was doing?"

"Everyone will know what we did today."

"The only ones coming back are Jeb and Yollie. They won't pay any attention."

"I'll be embarrassed."

"It'll be fine. Don't worry about it. Nobody made any comment about Julia and Ned."

"They're older."

"We're too young?"

She grinned. "No. I think we're shocking."

"I find you make me feel rather electric, too. Something is going on. I didn't know people could feel this way."

"How?"

So naturally he showed her and made her laugh again. "All those times you told me to lock my door, I thought you meant against everyone else. I should have known it was really just to keep you out."

"I meant for you to lock me in with you."

"Ohh!" she exclaimed in great realization. "I didn't understand that."

"It's very tough to explain things to women. They simply don't think the way a man does."

"No?" She gave him a salacious look, with heavy eyes and an inviting smile.

They finally went downstairs slowly, teasing, kissing, touching. Alone. And they went to the kitchen to see what they'd have for supper. They weren't terribly interested. They had the whole lodge to themselves, and the whole evening and night and morning free. In the kitchen, he told her, "I've wanted to back you up to that counter all week," and so he did, and he kissed her as he'd wanted to that entire time. She helped, with his hips holding hers firmly in place and the heels of his hands pressing into the sides of her breasts.

As if imparting information, she mentioned, "My tongue's getting tired from kissing."

"Like any muscle, it needs exercise."

"Somehow I figured you'd have a glib reply."

He touched his tongue to his upper lip and looked smug.

They opened a bottle of wine and took their glasses out onto the porch. They sat close and told each other how marvelous they were, and they kissed a whole lot. Soft, caressing kisses, not just to be kissing but to exercise her tongue. And they could finally talk about Bill.

"I wondered if he would leave." Logan watched her.

"Every once in a while, I've had guys act that way since I was twelve. It can be a real nuisance. I don't do anything. Mom says it's not unusual. It happens to most women more or less. Dad says men can have the same problem. He says it's my hair."

"And so you concealed it so I wouldn't be attracted."

"Yes."

"But that disguise didn't fool me—or Bill. He has good taste. I believe he's recently divorced. Maybe in the last year."

"And lonely," Kim said as she'd said before.

With Bill gone, Logan could be tolerantly surmising. "He'd like to start fresh. He's looked at his life, and it isn't the way he'd planned. He's still young, not yet in his prime, and he's restless, looking around. So here you are. A stunning young woman on the brink of life, not averse to being domestic, a great cook, a real trooper, and he saw in you a second chance, a better chance. I'm glad he left. I would hate to have to fight him over you. But I would. And if it came to... anything really serious, I don't know how far I would go to prevent him from touching you."

"I was so relieved he left. I wanted to be here, alone with you."

"God, Kim, I love you."

Their kiss was so profound that their heads buzzed. They pulled apart to look at each other, and the buzz continued to accelerate. They looked puzzled, then they frowned. It took a minute before they realized the sound they heard was that of a plane.

Nine

"A plane!" Kim was only surprised then, not at all alarmed.

"Why would anyone be flying in?" Logan asked. "If they intend to land, why haven't they called in?"

And Kim realized she, too, had been listening for the radio's betraying, crackling spurts. Her words slowed with Logan's questioning. "No one's expected. Jeb said that very clearly. That's why he felt he could leave."

"It's a single-engine." Logan labeled it. "If Jeb sent someone on up without him, we'll soon know. But it's odd they haven't radioed in."

"How do you know it's a single-engine?"

"It sounds different." He then named the type and make of the plane.

"How do you know that?"

"I fly."

"You never mentioned being a pilot."

"With my pretending to be nearly blind, I'd hardly mention flying!"

By then they were standing. They moved to the edge of the porch, but almost immediately Logan drew Kim back into the shadows. That's when she became uneasy.

Logan was thinking aloud. "If anyone was slated to come, Jeb wouldn't have left. If it's mail or supplies or whatever, they wouldn't be delivering it separately. There's nothing that couldn't wait for the trip tomorrow. This isn't normal. It would have to be something unusual. If someone needed gas or some kind of help, they would have called in by now." He didn't mention a third possibility.

"What would anyone steal here? There're supplies. Or maybe somebody's lost?"

"We'd have heard on the radio if someone was lost."

"Who on earth?"

"Until we know otherwise, we'll assume it's a dangerous person. We're alone."

How glad they'd been to be alone! But now fear licked through Kim's stomach. She felt trapped. No car to leap into and roar off. No one to call to. Just Logan, the pacifist, the antiwar, antiaggressive man. Her stare went to him, then her eyes widened in surprise. His stance was like a seriously angry bear whose territory was being challenged. The change in him startled Kim.

Logan said, "He has to make the flyover check. We
have time. Grab a good coat, gloves, extra socks. We'll
get some food. We might have to stay away from the
lodge for twenty-four hours. Then Jeb will be back
and will find us or get help. We'll go into the woods."

"We could lock ourselves in upstairs," Kim suggested.

"If it's someone dangerous, they could burn the
place down. Let's get away from here." He shook her
arm a little. "Now! Before they land."

She hurried inside, and he followed closely. They
went to the equipment closet and grabbed coats and
gloves—and a fisherman's creel—but Logan hastily
made the closet neat again. They ran up the stairs.

Logan explained, "Don't disturb our room. If it's
messy, they'll know someone was here, saw them and
escaped into the woods. If they're criminals, they
might feel they have to hunt us down. But if it's neat,
they could assume we're simply out somewhere, and
they could just leave. However, if they already know
we're here, they might think we're at the cove and wait
for us to come back. Either way will give us some
time."

As the plane buzzed along the lake's surface, making the sight run, Logan and Kim were stuffing extra
socks and another pair of shoes into their pockets and
into the creel. They snatched up extra pairs of sweatpants to add for warmth, but they didn't take the time
to put them on. They had to get away.

The plane's long turn took the sound farther as they
ran down the stairs to the kitchen to grab bread, cheese
and oranges, then a hiker's bag hastily filled with wa-

ter. Their preparations were normal, as such a retreat could be, until Logan took up field glasses, a fisherman's all-purpose knife—and a gun. He added extra shells to both their pockets. Doing that was sobering. It made the threat real to a man who had so recently been a pacifist.

Was there a threat? Logan wasn't taking any chances with Kim. As he'd learned long ago from his mother: don't be a victim. So it was better to look a little foolish than to have Kim snatched or killed.

They went out the back door and began their escape down the track's uneven truck ruts. Logan told her, "Slow down. We've done the most important part. We're alerted, we're prepared, and now we'll find out whether we need to be either. Take it easy. We'll watch."

With the plane's motor changing pitch as it came in for the landing, they paused in their own flight down the track while there was still a glimpse through the trees to the dock. They would see how the intruder acted, or they might see it was Jeb! They would know in a few minutes.

"We must be quiet."

"It could be all right?" She couldn't believe there could be danger. In their Eden?

"We'll soon see. The others will be back tomorrow. It'll be less than a day, if we have to hide out. Don't worry until we need to."

"I love you."

"Kim, I love you very much." His deep voice was serious, but he didn't turn toward her. He lifted the glasses to his eyes as the plane eased toward the pier.

Their tension crackled. Who would it be? And why had they come there? The lovers watched silently.

A man emerged. With the powerful glasses, Logan could see clearly. "He's alone."

The man moved to loop the line to the post on the dock. He lifted his head and looked around.

Logan's voice was almost soft. "It's . . . Bill."

"What!" Kim gasped in disbelief.

"Yes, I hadn't known he was a pilot, or I wouldn't have relaxed with him gone."

"Why did he come back? He must have forgotten something?"

"You."

"Oh, don't be silly. He's a grown man! He's a big businessman. He wouldn't be guilty of doing anything so ridiculous. There has to be a logical explanation."

"Men aren't always logical where women are concerned."

"Men aren't that emotional. I've read articles—"

"He's walking to the lodge."

Bill went out of sight. He had acted in a perfectly normal way. He hadn't seemed furtive. He'd walked as any confident man in ordinary circumstances. Why hadn't he called in on the radio? Why was he there?

"If he searches—" Logan talked in whispers now "—he'll probably go first to our cove. We'll go to that tangle of logs we saw down the track. We should be able to find a place inside it and be safe. The way it is, no large animal could get to us, and we'll be out of sight. I'll give you the gun. You have shells."

"Don't leave me," she whispered. "I can help. I know judo."

"I'm karate black belt. Mother again. I had no brothers or a dad, so I had to learn to take care of myself."

"Did you ever have to?"

"Not once. But I did assume the opening position once and—" He stopped and hissed, "Shh. Listen. I heard the front door."

From that distance, almost two city blocks, and unsettlingly clearly, they heard Bill call, "Kim!"

So Bill knew they weren't inside the lodge. With a dangerously lightened voice, Logan commented to no one, "How strange he isn't calling for me."

"He's bigger than you." She was dreading a confrontation.

"He doesn't know I can see."

"Ah." She breathed the word in understanding. "A secret weapon."

Logan looked down at Kim, close beside him, and asked her, "Aren't you glad we're out here and not locked inside that lodge?"

"Your mother is a wise woman."

"You'll like her, and after a while, you'll realize you love her, too."

"Kim!" Bill's call came again.

"How come he isn't interested in seeing me?"

"You're not redheaded."

"How can you be so sassy?" He was really surprised. "Aren't you afraid of him?"

"He wouldn't hurt me."

"Any man who would leave and then turn right around and come back here—all that way, in a plane big enough for two—is a threat to you. And he doesn't intend taking me along."

Her eyes widened. "How can you know that?"

"It's what I'd do."

"Nonsense."

"I wouldn't let another man touch you."

"I can take care of myself."

"You're to stay here with me." He wasn't entirely certain she'd obey.

"Of course."

"Kim!" The sound was different.

"It sounds as if he's going to the cove. Let's just ease on down the track and get to that log fall. Too bad it stays light so long. But it may take a while for him to search the track. He'll find the gun gone, but there are other guns in the lodge. Remember that."

"Don't do anything foolish or brave."

"I will if it's necessary; I intend for us to survive."

"Me, too."

They went as quietly as they could. The untidy track, with its spongy ground and carelessly tossed debris of branches and bark, wandered along, taking the path of least resistance. So they walked farther than a crow would fly that distance, but it was faster than going through the woods, and they didn't get lost.

They came to the snare of logs, and it seemed like a haven. They climbed up the logs and could find all sorts of nests inside it. Kim was so bent on hiding that she didn't consider if anything else had taken refuge there.

Quietly Logan instructed, "You get down so I can see if you're visible. But be sure you can see down the track. He'll be coming along it eventually. But he might come through the woods. I'll watch our backs."

"This can't be happening."

"It's only for a while. Jeb and Yollie will be back in less than twenty-four hours. Bill knows that, too. Let's not take any chances."

"It's just so incredible. I'm having trouble believing it." She tested one place and then climbed out to try another.

"If we were just about anywhere else, we could confront him. I hesitate to do that here."

"I understand." She eased into a crossed-beam nest. "This spot isn't bad. I feel as if we've found a stockade. I can see just fine—I can see the whole track until the trees block it. I can sit quite comfortably. Can you see me?"

"Not well. Let me see you move. Not bad. If he comes, hold still. If he should shoot into the pile, duck down. I'll handle it all."

"Do you really think... My God, Logan, would he actually shoot at us?"

"I doubt it." He soothed her. "I just want us to be prepared for whatever could happen."

"Where will you be?"

"Almost right behind you, there's a place." He climbed above her and smiled down at her. Then he moved down between the piled logs. When he was settled, they could reach through and touch. He took her hand and kissed it. "Now be quiet, get as comfortable as you can, watch and listen."

She folded the extra pants under her bottom. They divided the food and put the water bag between them on a log where both could reach it. They waited.

"When he gets back from the cove, he'll start looking around. He'll find the gun gone. And he'll know we're hiding."

"He might figure the bears got us."

"Not both of us. Bears love redheads, and I'd be in a tree."

"You take me along as bear bait?" She was indignant.

"Would there be another reason?"

"I suppose not."

"There is." His voice was husky.

"What?"

"I can't show you right now."

"Does it have to be shown?"

"Demonstrated," he corrected. "It's more fun than just telling."

"Try the telling."

"I had no idea how much I love you. I knew it, but the threat to you has . . . underlined it. If Bill comes here, he's going to think you had to lead me here."

"Yes."

"And that you're essentially alone. That I won't even be able to see him."

"Yes."

"Don't mention my sight."

"I'm smarter than that."

"You could say, 'Look! He's got a gun.'"

"We have one, but will he carry one, too?"

"I would imagine we'll find out."

She paused before she said slowly, "I couldn't shoot someone I know."

"What if he shot you?"

"I would be astonished."

"People can be quite vicious. These are strange times."

"All times are." She sighed. "I've read of other times, and there were problems with all sorts of things, just like now. The problems are always towering, and no one ever thinks they'll make it, but some do. Some have. They have to have survived, or we wouldn't be here."

"I hope we're slated to figure in the survival rate."

"You certainly should." She was positive. "Although you're tricky and glib, you're exceptional."

"So you love me."

"A little."

"How fortunate for you. Otherwise it could be difficult being my slave."

"I've noticed a definite tendency in you to revert to a strong masculine barbarism. *Is* it the woods? Or has this tendency just lain dormant, and now it's surfacing?"

The dinner triangle rang at the lodge. It was startlingly loud and carrying. It was chilling for her to realize Bill sought them. Why had he come there?

"It *is* time for supper," Logan commented. "Do you suppose he's annoyed you don't have his ready?"

"I have no appetite at all."

"It would be smart for us to nibble something now. Want an orange?"

She suggested, "Split one?"

"Go easy on the water."

"I'll be glad to find this has all been a farce. He'll come and say, 'Why did you hide? What was the purpose?' And we'll laugh."

"We'll see. Don't count on that until it happens."

"If he really isn't dangerous, our absence could alarm him. He could think we're in danger. Or dead."

"Maybe we just don't want to be disturbed."

"I almost wish he'd come and confront us so I could find out."

Logan said softly, "I imagine you'll get your wish." His voice sounded so dangerous Kim's flesh goosebumped.

They heard the dinner triangle sound again, loud and long.

"At least we know exactly where he is right this minute." Kim was becoming a little tense. "I could probably conjure up all sorts of phantoms out there in the woods. I'm glad I'm monitoring the track."

"The glasses help."

It was so still they heard Bill calling, "Come on out! I know you're here!"

"Ah." Logan breathed out the word. "That does settle things. He knows we're hiding. Thank God we're here."

"Maybe not. Maybe he just doesn't realize we might not be hiding. That something could have happened."

"I'm glad you're with me. If you'd been here alone, you'd have trustingly gone out on the pier to greet him, and you'd have walked right into his hands."

"Will he come looking for us?"

"Definitely. He's betrayed himself. He must be furious. He's thinking of you with me, and it's jarred his judgment."

"Logan, I can't see him that ensnared by me. He's only known me a week."

"So have I, my love."

"But I was encouraging you. Not Bill."

"You have to remember that you led me around and you took care of me but you didn't flirt with me either."

"I didn't think you could see me flirt," she told him.

"Right. But Bill didn't see you flirting with me either. And he knew why we were here. We had to stay. He could well believe I've dragged you off into the bushes and had my wicked way with you."

"You did."

"But you didn't appear to mind."

"I helped." Her voice was tender.

"I want you right now."

"Isn't that strange? I want you, too. I want to make love with you right this impossible minute."

There was a shot, which splintered the silence.

"He'll come." Logan's voice was hushed.

"Oh, Logan."

"He has to fly out before dark. Or wait for morning and risk being caught here. It's tricky to take off from a strange lake in the darkness, unless there'd be a moon. I wonder how skilled he is as a pilot.''

''I'm glad he doesn't have a dog,'' she whispered.

''Yes.''

''When will he try the track?''

''I don't know. He might look in the area around the lodge first. While he was here, he didn't explore the track that I remember. He was fishing. He might not realize how far it comes into the woods. It isn't distinct.''

''But there's the truck,'' she reminded him. ''A truck would only be needed for some distance.''

''Yes. But it's so dilapidated he might not realize how rugged it is or how far this track goes. And this week, if he should have noticed the truck, it was only as it was being worked on.''

''I'm . . .'' But she stopped.

''What's the matter? Do you see him?''

How could he sound so calm? ''I'm a little nervous.''

Logan gave a breathy ghost of a laugh. ''It's a nervous time.''

''I don't want you hurt.''

''Neither of us,'' he agreed. ''That's what we're trying to prevent.''

''*Kim!*'' Bill yelled.

He was still closer to the lodge.

Kim said hopefully, ''If we're very quiet, he might just go on by us.''

''If he's only a fisherman, that might be so, but even I saw these piled logs as a hiding place. He's a male.

Men look at things differently than a woman. I would bet that you looked on this snag as something to be cleaned up."

"Yes." She could admit that readily enough.

"I love you, Kimberly. Be very still. He could just go on by, but if he starts to investigate this pile, I'll have to stop him."

"I understand. But talk first. He would have a hard time getting us out of here."

"If he shoots, burrow down deep."

"I know. I would. I love you, Logan. Take care of yourself. Don't do anything valiant. I prefer a careful Logan—who is alive—to a brave dead one."

"I'll take care of you."

"That's a deliberately enigmatic reply."

"Shh. Listen."

They could hear him coming. Bill called out, and he wasn't being at all careful. He didn't care that they heard him. By the sounds Bill made as he came down the track, they could judge how far he was. Logan reached through the opening between them and said, "Courage."

Kim squeezed his hand. "I feel rather excited, in a 'hold-the-fort' sort of way. More excited than scared. I'm surprised that's so. How about you?"

"I'm not sure. 'Very serious' probably would describe it. I don't feel I'm playing King of the Mountain."

"That's my feeling exactly!" Kim's reply was a little excited.

"You sound like a woman who would catch an escaped fish with her bare hands...and then would make a pet of him. Whoever heard of a fish called Elmer?"

The sounds were coming closer. Kim's voice dropped to a hush, but she said, "When we get back, we'll let Elmer go."

She gave him her confidence that he could get them out of this mess. They would go back, and they would survive. It could work out to be a false alarm; but there were too many flaws in Bill's coming back for it to be just a friendly visit.

The two waited silently. Both now watched the track, since they knew Bill was alone and coming down the track toward them. They were holed up, waiting.

Logan was surprised that Kim's King of the Mountain feeling was edging into his instinct of prepared caution. He smiled to himself. And waited.

Ten

Bill came into sight. He was just a man. He wasn't as tall as the trees after all. He was as he had been, just a little over six feet. He was watching where he placed his feet, because he wore dress shoes that had slick soles. It was difficult footing, with the carelessly discarded branches, and the ground moss hampered smooth walking. But he carried a gun.

As Logan and Kim watched him, Bill looked up in a sweeping glance, and his eyes came to the tangle of logs. He stopped. He didn't look farther. He studied their stockade.

He called, "Kim." It really wasn't a question. It was as if he demanded to know why she was hidden from him and hadn't replied to his calls.

In only a breath of air, Logan warned her, "Hush."

The truck had never gone near the tangle, and with some irritation, Bill looked on the debris that littered the ground between him and the pile of logs, but he began to make his way closer.

Adrenaline surged into Logan's veins. He didn't want Bill too close, but he was coming forward, watching the ground, not dodging from tree to tree or even watching the tangle. Logan said with quiet threat, "That's far enough."

Bill's head snapped up. "So you are there. Kim?"

She heard Logan's quick intake of breath, but, having been warned so many times to be silent, Kim was.

"What have you done with her?" Bill demanded.

"She's safe."

"In whose opinion? Do you have her there with you?"

"Why are you here?"

"Where is she?" Bill began to move forward again, climbing over the debris. His temper was high, his movements a little rash as he scrambled toward their stockade in a grim determination.

"Stay back!"

"I know you have the gun. Do you intend to shoot me?"

"Why are you here?" Logan asked again with stern demand for a reply.

"Because I think you're a danger to her."

"I?" Logan's indignation was palatable.

"You may have fooled Kim and everyone else, but I believe you can see. Why would you pretend to be half blind? What have you done with Kim? Where is she? I don't know how Jeb could have agreed to leave her here with you. Where is . . ." He took another step on the tangle of debris, the slick soles of his shoes gave no help, and he fell.

In that stillness, even Logan and Kim heard the crack. A branch? His leg? They heard his first writhing exclamation. "Damn!"

"A trick." Logan was sure.

"No," breathed Kim.

"You're much too trusting."

"Bill?" she called.

"Well, thank God you're alive. Are you all right? What's he done to you?"

"Nothing." Well, nothing bad. "Are you all right?"

"I've busted my damned leg."

"How do we know that's true?" Logan demanded. "It could be a snare."

"What the hell do you mean?"

"Why didn't you call in before you landed?"

"The damned radio went out on me."

"We're supposed to believe you came all this way back just to check on Kim?"

"I left some papers here, but I only used that to justify my coming. I could have had them tomorrow. I had to be sure about Kim. She's too nice a girl for you to trick her that way. Kim, come help me."

Logan commanded, "Throw your gun away to your right."

"Now, why should I do that? For all I know, I've only interrupted you. Why do you have her clear out here? Hiding in a woodpile? What are you up to?"

"I'm protecting her from you."

"Me! What the hell are you talking about?"

"I'll go down," Kim said. "I'll stay out of your way, Logan, so you can have a clear shot at him. Then I can see if his leg is really broken. I heard a snap."

"It's broken." Bill was bent over it.

"He could have snapped a branch and just taken advantage of the sound."

Bill growled, "Someone as sly as you wouldn't trust anyone. You think everyone is rotten. Kim, come away from him. I'll take care of you."

"Sit still," Logan advised quietly. "I'll go."

Kim whispered, "No! He could shoot your head off as soon as you stood up."

Bill called, "Is he giving you trouble?"

"No, I'm coming down."

"Kim! Sit still!" Logan stood up.

Kim quickly stood in front of him. "Don't shoot!" she called to Bill. "I'm coming down."

Logan put his gun to his shoulder and took close aim on Bill.

Bill stared at Logan. "A blind man with a gun on me? I've never seen such a farce!"

Logan replied coolly, "Telescopic lens."

Bill grunted in disgust, then groused at Kim, "Why the hell would I shoot you? Be careful, for God's sake! Do you want to break your leg, too?"

"I'm young and more flexible."

"I don't need any snide remarks about my age. I hurt like hell as it is. Get over here and tell me you're all right."

"I'm fine." She had moved to his gun side, keeping out of Logan's line of fire. "Which leg?"

"The one at the odd angle." His tone was a little nasty.

He was exaggerating. But his eyes showed the pain, and his teeth were clenched. He didn't offer to move. If he was faking a broken leg, he should get accolades for acting. She called back, "Logan, it's really broken. We have to get him to help." She took the gun from by his hand and pitched it away.

Bill growled in irritation, "And how the hell do you plan to get help?"

She looked at Logan, who continued to appear hampered by poor sight and was coming carefully down the tangle of woods. She echoed Bill: "How are we going to get him to help?"

"Can't we just leave him here?" Logan smiled at Kim.

"No." She smiled back. If Bill had been an enemy, he was defanged.

"It was stupid of you to come back." Logan stood looking down at Bill critically.

"Yes," Kim added. "You should have realized I wouldn't have stayed alone with Logan if I had any reason to be afraid of him."

"You're defenseless. He's bigger than you. You shouldn't trust him. I believe he's a trickster."

Miffed, Kim said, "I know what I'm doing."

"You're too young to judge men correctly."

Annoyed he'd think her a child, she snapped, "At your age, you should know better than that." She was a little snooty.

Angrily Bill retorted, "Quit putting me into a wheelchair! I'm not that old."

Logan took it up. "A wheelchair is exactly what we need. I could lug him out, but it's a long way, and he's bigger than I." He smiled again.

"I'm thirty-eight." Bill was still mad at Kim but defending himself to her.

"That's only a year or two younger than my dad would be," Kim said to put him in his place.

But Logan took up for Bill and said in kindly explanation, "She's just trying to tell you—"

And Bill said, "Shut up!"

Kim saw that Bill had a film of sweat on him from pain. The break wasn't a compound fracture—it was a simple one—but the bone was broken, and it hurt.

Logan touched Kim's arm. "Honey, you'll have to be the one to get the truck. Can you drive it okay?"

"I'll manage." She looked down at Bill. "I'll be back as soon as I can."

Logan moved, then instead he asked, "Where's Bill's gun? You need to carry it along. Be careful."

Kim took up the gun, feeling extremely brave and pioneerish. "I'll be back." She started off. Turning once, she looked back. Logan watched her until she was out of sight.

Bill prodded tartly, "You're not going to leave me here to rot?"

"Not this time." Logan squatted down. "How can I make you more comfortable?"

"Don't move me until we have to."

"Kim belongs to me."

"If you harm her, I'll break your neck."

"I love her," Logan told him.

"In a week? Undying devotion?"

"From the minute she got off that plane with her tricolored hair, that green lipstick and gold cheeks. Irresistible."

"How'd you see all that?"

Logan laughed in his throat. "I had my glasses then. I could see everything." He still told only the truth.

"She took my eye," Bill admitted.

"You made that pretty clear," Logan agreed.

"Too bad neither of us smokes. This is when the villain gives the hero a cigarette."

Logan lifted his brows. "I suspect you are casting me in the villain's role?"

"How'd you figure that out?"

"You're a hero type. When I'm your age, I hope I can be like you."

Disgruntled, Bill groused, "Insults aren't needed right now. I'm not that old."

"I meant it as a compliment. You're twelve very important years older than I. You've made your mark. You'll be an impact on your business in these next twenty-five or thirty years. I'm impressed by you. And I'm impressed that you came back to check on Kim. Of course—" his voice was humorous "—when I saw who had landed, uninvited and unannounced, you unsettled me a little."

"Yes, I can see how that would be. I'd have probably reacted just the way you did. You were very smart to get her out of the lodge. I hadn't looked at it from your point of view."

"I wasn't sure of your intentions."

With an irascible look, Bill admitted, "I would take her from you."

"Thank God you broke your leg."

From the distance, they could hear Kim starting the truck with loud grindings and bangs. Then the motor settled down to a rasping, hiccuping roar.

"She's okay so far." Logan rose to his feet to look down the track. "We might have to back all the way out. There's no turnaround. I wonder if she noticed that." He looked down at Bill. "She'll be here soon."

"Don't be too quick to cheer for my broken leg. Women can be very tender to a disabled man, as you must know—you've worked your flawed sight to the nth degree."

Logan grinned. "One does as one must."

"Don't be so damned likable. I prefer to think you're crafty and disagreeable."

"I would be very dangerous to any man who tried for Kim." He said the threatening words quite casually.

Bill grinned.

The sound of the truck came closer. "She's almost here. In just a minute we'll have you aboard. It'll be a hell of a trip to the lodge. Very rough."

"No choice." Bill accepted the situation.

"We'll try to wedge you so you won't jounce too much."

"I appreciate your efforts."

"I'll call a price," Logan told Bill softly.

"Oh?"

"Stay away from Kim. You could nudge me out with very little effort."

"She thinks I'm too old," Bill groused.

"She isn't yet of the mind to marry. She's getting there, but when she does decide she's ready, I don't want you anywhere around."

"If I refuse, you'll leave me here?" Bill was caustic.

"I'd be surprisingly tempted, but my conscience will force me to help you. If you are grateful, back away from Kim."

"God, I'm tempted not to."

"I sympathize." Logan gave Bill that much.

"Why did you have to turn out the way you are?"

"I haven't changed. You only know me now. I've known the threat of you all along."

"She's very special," Bill said seriously.

"So was Tate."

"Tate?"

"You really have a case on Kim if you didn't notice Tate." Logan shared that wisdom.

"If you noticed her, does that mean you have a roving eye?"

"No, I only saw Tate as a woman, not as a potential lover."

"She was one of the two women."

Logan elaborated. "Yes. Julia was with Ned."

"I remember."

"You sound as if you saw them weeks ago."

Bill sighed. "It's been a very long day."

"Well, I can understand that. Kim will be here soon."

"I wish you weren't here."

Logan asked practically, "If I weren't, how would you get in the truck?"

"Yeah."

Logan stood up, looking toward the sound of the approaching truck.

Bill watched him. "It's almost as if you can see."

Logan didn't look at Bill, but he smiled. "I have excellent hearing." That was true.

The sound of the truck burst from the screening of the trees. She was backing in. Good girl, Logan thought. Driving forward as they returned to the lodge, they could choose their route better for the sake of Bill's leg.

Bill exclaimed, "She's backed all this way, bless her."

Logan didn't reply. He called, "Are you okay?"

"I'm here. This truck is the *pits*! Jeb ought to junk it."

"Beggars—"

"I know!" she snapped. "I *know*!"

Logan said in an aside to Bill, "Terrible disposition." But he grinned. "Redheaded woman."

Bill said, "I wouldn't mind."

Kim eased the truck closer, watching out the cab door and turning to look the other way.

Logan asked Bill, "Is her way clear?"

Bill groaned as he raised his head to look. "Tell her to stop. That log could hang up the truck."

"Hold it! Bill says there's a log in your way."

She gave Logan an impatient glare for continuing his sham, but she stopped. She hopped out of the cab and came toward them.

Logan congratulated her. "Bill says you backed in. Brilliant."

She just gave him an impatient look.

Bill said, "You washed your hair...for him."

She'd taken off her cap, but she'd forgotten she was no longer four colored. She said nothing in reply to Bill but asked Logan, "How do we do this?"

"How's the truck bed?" He went over and felt around. "Honey, let's fix a couple of logs to brace him so he won't roll so badly."

"Okay. Which ones?"

"I don't want you to lift them. Just choose the ones you think will do. If they have some bracing limbs, they'll be better. Then they won't roll."

She looked around, and it all looked like a mess to her. But Bill took an instant interest. "How about that one?"

Logan said, "Here?"

"No, to your left."

Kim narrowed her eyes. This was silly. Bill was no threat. Why did Logan have to act this way? Rather roughly, she went to Logan, turned his arm and pulled him down to the log. He grinned at her, very amused. She could have kicked him.

Bill chose the other logs, too, and Kim directed Logan to the correct ones. Logan lifted them effortlessly, fitted them into the truck bed, then went to Bill and said, "This might not be fun."

"I know. But it beats staying here."

Kim put her and Logan's coats and the spare sweatpants onto the truck to pad Bill's slot between the logs. Logan snugly splinted Bill's leg, stood him on his good leg, then carried him in the fireman rescue hold to the back of the truck. There, he again stood Bill on his good leg, then got up on the truck and lifted him to sit on the edge, then helped him into the slot. They were both sweating by then: Bill from pain; Logan from compassion. They cushioned his leg, and Logan said, "I'll ride back here, honey, to be sure the logs don't crowd him. Take it easy on the bumps."

She gave Logan a wide-eyed stare, then she flipped around and went back to drive to the lodge. She was careful. She took the time to be as easy as she could. It was a hellish trip for Bill, but they did make it.

"Now what?" Bill asked.

"I'll take a look at that radio, and we'll fly out."

"Wait a minute. There's no way I can fly a plane with a broken leg."

"How fainthearted you are!" Logan expressed great astonishment.

"Don't be cute." Bill's voice was a snarl.

"I can't help it."

Bill directed, "Kim, go inside and try the radio. See if you can get a rise out of anyone qualified to look at me."

Logan said soothingly, "I'll fly us out."

"Yeah. Sure."

"No problem. I've driven a car. A plane can't be too different." Logan stood surveying the shed as if it were the plane.

Kim almost laughed. Logan was being very, very wicked. He was about to scare Bill witless. How far should she let him go with this?

They left Bill on the truck, and Kim pretended to lead Logan into the shed for the tool kit. "What are you doing?"

Completely logical, Logan replied, "I'm keeping his mind off his leg."

"Well, I guess you are! But, Logan, you could give him a heart attack!"

Logan had the kit, turned and left the shed with Kim hurrying along beside him. In a low voice Logan promised, "He'll know by the time we get off the lake. He'll know he can trust me."

She hissed back, "You didn't trust him."

"I still don't. Not with you. As a man, he's superior. But as a competitor, he's low, sneaky and untrustworthy."

"He isn't competing."

Logan smiled. "Trust me."

"Ah, yes, my blind pilot friend, I have every reason to trust you."

Logan assured her, "He'll tell this story all the rest of his life."

"You will, you mean."

"Well, I might mention it a time or two." They had arrived on the dock by the plane.

"You're outrageous." She shook her head.

"I'm the victor hero."

"You are, you know."

"Kiss me. He's watching. I want him to be grim."

She wrapped her arms around him, leaned into his body and kissed him with fervor.

He eased away from her and coughed a little. "I didn't mean for you to double-whammy me. I have to fix the radio and remove one seat. You do that again, and I'll drag you off into the bushes and forget Bill altogether."

She promised, "I'll behave."

"Only temporarily."

"Yes, sir."

"There you go again, demanding my attention!"

"Sorry."

"You just have to be careful. You know I'm susceptible."

She said again, but with a big grin, "I'll behave."

"Well," he said grudgingly, "one more."

She kept her hands behind her back, but his made up for her lack, and he kissed her until her brain cells forgot their normal places. He released her busily, but she leaned a hand on the plane for a while and just looked down toward the dock. While she was deciding which side was up, Logan whistled cheerfully as he tinkered with the radio. It was only a loose wire, easily secured. Then he used a wrench to remove the second seat.

"I'll stay here—until you get back." Even her own hearing confirmed how mournfully brave she sounded.

"No, you're going along. We'll fit."

They did. They found the papers Bill had deliberately forgotten, but Bill objected strongly to being carried aboard a plane to be flown off a lake by a man who was practically blind.

Logan said crossly, "Hold still!"

"You'll kill us all. You can't do this." Bill was positive.

"Be quiet. I can. I've always heard pilots say they fly by the seat of their pants. I can at least use my hands and feet."

"Kim!" Bill demanded her assistance.

Kim smiled. "I trust Logan."

"Good Lord. Can't I talk you out of this?"

"Nothing ventured, nothing gained." Logan arranged Bill on the cockpit floor, and Kim sat by him.

Bill urged, "Kim, don't come along. If he is determined to kill us both, you stay here."

"I really trust him." She spoke with confidence.

"On the floor like this, I can't even see." Bill was agitated.

She smiled and winked at Bill. She simply couldn't stand for him to be so alarmed. Bill gave her a hard look, and she returned it serenely. So then Bill watched Logan like a hawk. Logan settled himself in the seat with an odd familiarity, put on headphones, turned on the radio and called in. Then he checked instruments with a knowledgeable flick, and Bill saw that. Casting a glance at Kim, who smiled back, Bill said, "He can see."

"Like an eagle," Kim told him.

Filled with virtue, Logan admonished Bill, "All's I did was pay you back for the blood I sweat when you landed unannounced."

Bill growled, "I could wring your damned neck."

The motor idled as Logan continued checking, identifying himself, asking directions. Then with skill, he eased the plane from the dock, moved it out onto the lake, turned, revved up the engine to full pitch and took off beautifully. Bill said, "This is as close as you're ever going to get to heaven."

Logan laughed.

They flew Bill west to Red Lake; it was closest. They were met, and Bill was put into a van, his eyes never leaving Kim, and he was driven away to the hospital.

Logan refueled, picked up a pilot to return the plane to its home base and flew them back to Jeb's lake. The two men reset the second seat, and with plenty of time until the eleven-o'clock dusk, the pilot flew off, leaving the pair on the dock.

They looked at each other and smiled. "I'm starved," she said, and Logan kissed her. It was a different kiss. Not greedy. If a kiss could show commitment, that one did. Kim recognized it was so. "Logan, I still have a year of school."

"We'll handle that."

"How do we know this isn't propinquity? We're the only two our age here. We could just be mesmerized by biology and isolation."

"We'll go slowly," Logan soothed her.

"In a week, look how far we've come."

"Aren't you sure of me?"

Kim replied, "Oddly enough, I am."

"Then . . . are you unsure?"

"Not right now."

"The time will come when you'll be positive." He was so assured. "Then we'll get married and live happily ever after, with a few spicy quarrels and a great deal of love."

"One of the problems is that you don't look like a domesticated man. Not anymore. I thought you were at first, that you were tamed and settled, but you aren't really civilized. I have to get used to you again."

"We have another week here." He grinned down at her, then deliberately looked at her hair. "You're different, too."

"Yes." She laughed.

"You're gorgeous. I need you right now."

"On the dock?" she teased.

"Let's try it on a bed." He said it as if being struck by an innovative idea. "We might have to work to adjust to a bed if we only make love on the ground or on a dock."

"Brilliant!"

They returned Jeb's truck to its place, and it coughed into silence as if it had died. They shook their heads and smiled. "At least it worked when we needed it," Logan commented. They went into the lodge and on upstairs to their room. They took off their clothes, showered and almost didn't make it back to the bed, because his kisses were steaming by then and his hands were feverish.

She said firmly, "Bed."

"Not the shower wall?"

"Bed." She was positive.

"Redheaded women are spoiled." He was very surprised.

"So are blue-eyed, black-haired men."

"Not yet. But I'm willing to be."

"How?"

"By you." He'd dried her carefully, then he rubbed the towel over himself very roughly but kept his eyes on her. She watched him with a slight smile and a vivid blush. He asked, "What are you thinking to blush so fiercely?"

"Bed."

He laughed with delight. "You win." He picked her up and carried her into their room, closed the door and locked it.

"Why lock it? We're alone here."

"I don't intend opening the door for several days. It's been a long day."

"I'm glad Bill wasn't a danger."

"I don't want to talk about Bill."

"Oh? What shall I talk about, then?"

"How much you love me."

"About—" she measured an almost-nothing slit between her thumb and forefinger "—that much."

Logan groused, "What a cold woman you are! I'll have to get your heat up, or you'll scorch when my hot love touches you. It's called equalizing pressure."

"Show me."

He laid her on the bed, but first he only looked at her. She smiled and put her arms up along her shoulders in an instinctive symbolic surrender that almost made him dizzy.

He moved to her and kissed her, holding her, and he'd been right about his heat. His hands and his body burned against the coolness of her skin. Shivers of excitement ran through her in so many ways, touching sensitive places and causing her to breathe differently and curl her body without ever knowing she did that to entice him.

She wanted him to be pleased, but he was working for her pleasure. Their sighs and sounds were enflaming to each other, and their touches were magic, causing feverish quiverings in their bodies, both in giving and in receiving doubled pleasure. Their skins became extremely sensitive, so that each kiss, each touch, was magnified, and their coupling was exquisitely sweet and thrilling. Their passion was pitched to the ultimate, and they rode a wild wind to completion.

Then they slept. They wakened to find each other and to love each other as they would for the rest of their lives. And they laughed and went downstairs in his shirts and their own jeans, to eat a supper in the darkness of the brief night. They drank a toast of love to their fathers, who were brilliant, and they became very sentimental over those long-ago men, whose legacy had interfered with their lives so beautifully.

*   *   *   *   *

Find out more about Tate in Silhouette Desire #437,
GOLDILOCKS AND THE BEHR,
coming out in July 1988.
Don't miss it!

Silhouette Romance ™

Legendary Lovers Trilogy

BY DEBBIE MACOMBER....

ONCE UPON A TIME, in a land not so far away, there lived a girl, Debbie Macomber, who grew up dreaming of castles, white knights and princes on fiery steeds. Her family was an ordinary one with a mother and father and one wicked brother, who sold copies of her diary to all the boys in her junior high class.

One day, when Debbie was only nineteen, a handsome electrician drove by in a shiny black convertible. Now Debbie knew a prince when she saw one, and before long they lived in a two-bedroom cottage surrounded by a white picket fence.

As often happens when a damsel fair meets her prince charming, children followed, and soon the two-bedroom cottage became a four-bedroom castle. The kingdom flourished and prospered, and between soccer games and car pools, ballet classes and clarinet lessons, Debbie thought about love and enchantment and the magic of romance.

One day Debbie said, "What this country needs is a good fairy tale." She remembered how well her diary had sold and she dreamed again of castles, white knights and princes on fiery steeds. And so the stories of Cinderella, Beauty and the Beast, and Snow White were reborn....

Look for Debbie Macomber's *Legendary Lovers* trilogy from Silhouette Romance: *Cindy and the Prince* (January, 1988); *Some Kind of Wonderful* (March, 1988); *Almost Paradise* (May, 1988). Don't miss them!

SRT-1

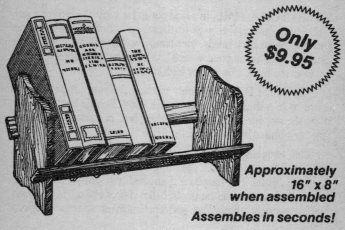

Silhouette Desire

COMING NEXT MONTH

AVAILABLE NOW:

Silhouette Intimate Moments

THIS MONTH
CHECK IN TO
DODD MEMORIAL HOSPITAL!

Not feeling sick, you say? That's all right, because Dodd Memorial isn't your average hospital. At Dodd Memorial you don't need to be a patient—or even a doctor yourself!—to examine the private lives of the doctors and nurses who spend as much time healing broken hearts as they do healing broken bones.

In UNDER SUSPICION (Intimate Moments #229) intern Allison Schuyler and Chief Resident Cruz Gallego strike sparks from the moment they meet, but they end up with a lot more than love on their minds when someone starts stealing drugs—and Allison becomes the main suspect.

In May look for AFTER MIDNIGHT (Intimate Moments #237) and finish the trilogy in July with HEARTBEATS (Intimate Moments #245).

Author Lucy Hamilton is a former medical librarian whose husband is a doctor. Let her check you in to Dodd Memorial—you won't want to check out!